TERROR STRIKES

To Chief Inspector Sharkey, the first murder is baffling enough: on a night-club dance floor, a man suddenly begins to choke. Horrified onlookers watch as he collapses and dies. It is quickly established that he has been strangled by someone standing directly behind him. But witnesses all testify that there was no one near him to do it. When this death is followed by a whole string of similar murders, Sharkey begins to seriously wonder if Scotland Yard is up against something supernatural . . .

NORMAN FIRTH

TERROR STRIKES

Complete and Unabridged

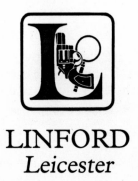

LINFORD
Leicester

First published in Great Britain

First Linford Edition
published 2015

A catalogue record for this book is available
from the British Library.

ISBN 978–1–4448–2520–6

Published by
F. A. Thorpe (Publishing)
Anstey, Leicestershire

Set by Words & Graphics Ltd.
Anstey, Leicestershire
Printed and bound in Great Britain by
T. J. International Ltd., Padstow, Cornwall

This book is printed on acid-free paper

1

The Terror Strikes

Soft, shaded lights beat down on the dance floor of the fashionable Elite-Splenda night club. The ten-piece orchestra beat out a foxtrot rhythm, while their coloured crooner mumbled husky words into the microphone. Waiters in evening dress navigated themselves and their loaded trays between the tightly packed tables with a dexterity born of long and assiduous practice. It was a proud boast of the club whose waiters had never been so utterly clumsy as to spill soup down the necks of the guests — so far. It was a scene that might have been observed any night, in any of London's classier night spots, where dukes rub elbows with movie stars, and barons jostle big-business moguls.

Señor Caleni Ventura ordered dinner for himself and his latest 'amour', doing mental arithmetic to estimate the total cost of the evening. Señor Ventura, although the possessor of millions of dollars, was always careful about little things like hotel bills, dinner charges, taxis, etc. It was a part of his natural Mexican cupidity, for Señor Ventura hailed from that country. He was thin-featured, typical of the inter-breeding of Indian and Spanish blood. His nose was fine and aquiline, his eye-brows black and heavy, his eyes rather protuberant. His hair was high back on his forehead, frizzy, and jet black.

Such, at forty, was Señor Caleni Ventura, late of Mexico City, now a director in the English firm of Public Promotions Ltd. He had arrived in England some ten years back, with the remnants of his father's legacy. He had heard that there were a lot of what he termed 'suckers' in England, and Señor Ventura looked on suckers as God's gift to Señor Ventura. His own money, and that of five other astute businessmen he had encountered, had floated their first venture, which was still going strong, and in which they held all the shares. There was little they wouldn't stoop to, and by way of a start they put on the market a new perfume, the formula of which Señor Ventura brought with him from his native country. It had sold by the gallon. It cost, actually, only a few pence a pint to manufacture; bottling and distribution brought the total cost to less than a pound an ounce, and the ounce bottle retailed in the most exclusive shops at twenty pounds.

Money had rolled in, and from there Public Promotions Ltd. had gone on to bigger and better things. Anything likely to prise some loose change off the suckers was tried: face powders, shaving lotions, remedies for baldness, and a hundred other things. Most of them had been fraudulent or harmful. Ventura and his comrades had been warned five or six times by the English law. But as rapidly as the law forced one commodity from the market, the señor stepped in with flashing teeth and smiling eyes and foisted some other fake on the unsuspecting public. He thrived, and the suckers went on buying, like suckers always do.

There was one thing, and one thing

only, which Public Promotions Ltd. had produced, and which *did* benefit the public. It was the wonderful and unbelievable cure for common colds, which sold at five pounds a bottle under the name of Shiftit Quick. It did cure colds, caught in time. Whence it had come, no one knew. Señor Ventura insisted it had been perfected in his own laboratories, and so it may have been. And on the strength of their faith in that solitary product, the public went on buying anything and everything that Ventura put on the market, good or bad — and it was invariably bad!

Therefore, as he gazed over the table with that amorous look in his eyes which many of his past flames knew too well, he was feeling eminently at peace with the world, and thought of his millions of suckers almost kindly. One of these suckers — only with a different meaning to the word — was before him now. Fay Marsden, twenty-five, a gold-digger type, with the face of an angel and the mind of a street woman, looked in turn at Ventura.

She knew perfectly well what he was

thinking. He was thinking that after the club closed he'd suggest a nightcap at his apartments and then, when she was good and drunk, would suggest she stayed the night. But this time Fay Marsden intended to out-wolf Ventura. It was her intention to get him drunk; then, with the licence she had taken care to get five weeks ago, to lug him to the nearest parson and get the ceremony performed. It would work all right if she could ram sufficient liquor down his throat. After which she would have one hell of a time seeing how fast she could spend the money he made. Which would be pretty fast at that.

'The dinner was most enjoyable, was it not, my flower?' said Ventura in his finest tone of voice. He caressed her hand, which he held beneath the tablecloth; and, encouraged by her passivity, allowed his fingers to wander coaxingly on to her silk-clad knee. A well-worn phrase ran through Fay's mind to the effect of, 'Latins are lousy lovers!' She found herself in complete agreement. Señor Ventura's methods would not have won the approbation of a harlot, even much less a young lady from the chorus of the *Night Life Follies*, currently running at the best theatres.

But she smiled and said, 'It was lovely, señor. It's so good of you to keep asking me out and never expect anything at all from me in payment.'

Ventura grunted. This was an unprofitable line of thought. He had no desire to assume the proportions of a big-brother type. He said, 'Ah, no, *mia*. I am not like that. But — at some times I find myself almost carried away by your exquisite beauty, my love. There are times when the señor must keep a tight grip upon his emotions, lest he press you suddenly, madly, to him, and cover your fair face with kisses.'

'Oh, *señor*!'

'Call me Caleni,' he whispered. 'I hoped that tonight we might slip round to my apartment? I have some excellent wine there.'

She laid her hand on his and gently but firmly removed it. She said, 'I would like that, Caleni,' and she dropped her eyes demurely.

The band struck up a further number,

a waltz this time. Couples drifted aimlessly onto the floor, jammed into a knot, and began to shuffle feet and waggle hips at each other. This passed for dancing at the Elite Splenda on a crowded night.

Ventura said, 'Shall we — er — go and stand with the rest on the dance floor, my dear? It will at least give me an excuse for holding your adorable body in my arms.'

Fay nodded, and hoisted the aforementioned adorable body from its chair. Ventura clasped her tightly to him, waited for an opening on the floor, saw one, and inserted himself into it.

Ventura sighed dutifully, and they managed to gyrate four paces forward and four backward. A bony elbow jabbed Fay in the back; a nattily garbed foot landed on Ventura's corn. His features screwed up in agony.

'What's the matter, dear? Aren't you well?' Fay asked.

Ventura nodded reassuringly. He could hardly talk about his corns at a time like this. He said, 'I am in excellent health, my love — as you will shortly see for yourself.'

The orchestra had begun an encore;

clasped tightly together, they drifted round the floor. The lights suddenly changed to a mysterious green, concealing the minor details of the dancers. Señor Ventura immediately gave his hands full play, to the accompaniment of shocked giggles and ineffectual protests from his lady.

'Oh, Caleni, you mustn't,' she protested half-heartedly, and he smiled down at her.

And, then suddenly, for no visible reason, his face changed. It changed *horribly*. A look of surprise spread over it first; this quickly changed to fear and pain. Fay said, 'Señor! Have you — has someone trod on your foot?'

He didn't answer her; only strangled gurgles left his lips. His already jutting eyes protruded far out, as if they were on stalks. Panic glimmered in his reddish-brown pupils. His eyebrows curled up as his forehead wrinkled. He looked like a man in the last stages of some terrible horror. His hands left her, reached up for his throat and tore savagely away at empty air. Horrible gagging sounds left his lips . . . His mouth opened gaspingly, his tongue began to emerge . . . Farther and farther it came, sickening the bewildered girl; he seemed to be trying to say something to her, but only choked gasps came.

Fay screamed in sudden terror. Her first idea had been that he was having a fit, but now she could see this was not so. Her scream ended in little sobbing noises; her eyes were fixed rigidly on the ghastly green-tinted face of the amorous Señor Ventura.

As her scream rang out, the orchestra stopped playing. Suddenly the lights went on, and simultaneously Ventura fell to the floor and writhed helplessly, his tongue protruding ever farther.

The dancers stood petrified, unable to move or help. Ventura's eyes closed, then opened again . . . His gaze became fixed and glassy. Suddenly his hands dropped to the floor with two little thuds. His legs, twitching more slowly now, were motionless.

The manager of the club hurried through the crowd, cursing under his breath. He hated people throwing fits in his establishment. Most inconsiderate of them, he thought. Damned indecent, in fact.

He knelt by the now prostrate body and, as if their trance had suddenly snapped, the other dancers surged round in a mass. The head waiter pushed through and shouted, 'Stand back — give the man air. Haven't you ever seen a man in a fit before today?'

The manager stood up slowly, his face grey. He turned to the head waiter and said, 'Don't let anyone out of this room — lock the doors until the police arrive.'

'The — the police?' stammered the waiter.

'Yes — this isn't any fit. This man's been *strangled*!'

⋆   ⋆   ⋆

Chief Inspector Ebenezer Sebastian Sharkey lodged his plump rear on a handy chair and stared at the dancer-diners confronting him. Methodically, he extracted a match from his waistcoat pocket, pared the end into a point, and gouged culinary refuse from between his prominent teeth. Then, resting his right hand on his rotund paunch in a manner familiar to all who had come into contact with him, he said, 'I refuse to believe it. It's impossible! There's a man lying dead on the floor, with the bruises caused by the hands that choked him to death round his neck! He exhibits every aspect of a man murdered by strangulation. And yet, you who happened to be near him at the time insist there wasn't anyone at all strangling him! Either you're all blind or you're all mad — or I'm mad and this is all a delusion. Think again . . . '

'I can swear no one touched him,' said the peroxided blonde in the bosom-revealing gown. 'No one was even looking at him when it started.'

'Who're you?' asked Sharkey, spitting a portion of chewed matchstick onto the floor.

'I was dancing with him,' explained the girl. 'My name is Fay Marsden — we were going to be married.'

'Oh, you were, eh? Maybe *you've* got a jealous lover who did this? Could *that* be it?'

The girl stormed, 'Don't be a fool, officer. Do I look like the type of girl who has lovers?'

'*Exactly*,' nodded Sharkey unemotionally. He sighed and heaved his enormous bulk from the chair, which creaked gratefully. He went over to the body and drew aside the tablecloth which covered it. He said, 'Well, it isn't *me* who's seeing things. The marks are still there.'

'Perhaps,' suggested the manager nervously, 'he went into a fit, and strangled himself?'

Sharkey eyed him as if he were some interesting grub which had crawled out of a piece of cheese. He said, 'I don't think it happened in this case — but it's an idea! Why don't you try it some time?'

The manager subsided.

Sharkey continued: 'No man would be able to strangle himself completely — he'd lose the strength needed before he could finish the job. Besides, there are imprints of fingers on this man's throat — and the fingers happen to be indicating that he was gripped from behind. What does that give us?'

'Hypnotism?' suggested the manager brightly, bobbing up again with a natural resiliency.

Sharkey groaned and clutched his few remaining hairs. He moaned feebly: 'The same thing applies. Even if someone had used hypnotism or auto-suggestion on him, he still would have lacked the strength to actually strangle himself. No, that won't do. There must have been someone behind him — perhaps you didn't see them in the dim lighting you said was being used at the time?'

'That's possible — but when the lights went up again he was still choking on the floor, and everyone can testify there was no one strangling him!'

There was a chorus of assent from the crowd. Sharkey mopped perspiration from his brow, pared a further match and picked vigorously at his teeth. He said resignedly, 'All right, all right! You all say no one killed the man — you all swear no one was near him to do it. Yet he lies there, clearly strangled by two hands — which weren't his own. Now who's crazy? *You* or *me*?'

Fay Marsden faltered, 'I know how it looks, but we aren't mad. If anyone had been anywhere near him at all I would have known it. He was all right one minute, and the next . . . ' She shuddered and went on, 'If — if you ask me, there's something funny about the whole thing.'

'That's putting it mildly,' said Sharkey sarcastically.

'Something,' she went on, ignoring him, '*supernatural*!'

2

Collins Steps In

'A, er, *gentleman* to see you, sir,' said Miss Volt, sounding rather dubious about the 'gentleman' part of it.

Denby Collins, writer, glanced up from his hardboiled egg and said, 'What kind of a gentleman, Miss Volt? Gentlemen don't go about disturbing innocent citizens at this ungodly hour.'

'He gave his name as Chief Inspector Sharkey of Scotland Yard,' said Miss Volt, wrinkling her tip-tilted nose slightly, as if there was something unsavoury about the mere mention of a policeman.

Denby Collins suddenly grinned and said, 'Sharkey? Good God, he's no gentleman — more like a cross between an elephant and a boa constrictor. Show him in, Miss Volt. He's a member of the Curzon Crime Club, and one can't turn away club members, even if they aren't gentlemen. Roll him along.'

Miss Volt's trim, curvaceous figure vanished, to be replaced by the elephantine physique of Chief Inspector Sharkey. Sharkey stood in the doorway, chewing the inevitable matchstick, and regarded his fellow clubman. 'I heard your remarks about me,' he said in the tone of a small boy who has been mentally hurt.

'Then you shouldn't listen. There's an old adage which says listeners never hear good of themselves, but I suppose policemen are practically born with their ears to keyholes. Sit down and unload your feet; it must be tiring carrying that bulk about with you all day.'

Sharkey advanced into the room, sat down at the table, and looked at Denby's eggs with the stare of a man to whom eggs are an obsession. Denby politely rang a bell and a neatly clad maid appeared in the doorway. He said, 'Bring about half a dozen eggs for my friend, will you, Lorna?'

'Half a dozen, sir?' she said, incredulous.

Denby reflected and said, 'No — on second thought, better make it the round dozen.' Looking rather dazed, the maid disappeared.

Sharkey grunted and said, 'I didn't come here to feed my face, Collins.'

'I expect not — but you looked at my egg like a mother at her firstborn, and I suspected there were some bidden influences at work in your, er, brain, which made you yearn for eggs. I recall the way you can polish off food at the club dinners, my dear chap. So now you're here you must stay for an egg or two.'

Sharkey growled, 'Nor did I come here to be insulted.'

Denby made a delicate crack in his second eggshell, then scooped the top off neatly. He said, 'Pass the toast, Inspector — and tell me, why you did come here? It's rather revolting to a man of my sensitivity to have large, flat-footed minions of the law galloping about the place so early in the day. So unburden your mind.'

'Very well. I actually came to you for advice.'

'What kind of advice? How to live on a chief inspector's salary? How to reduce a fifty-inch waistline to thirty-two in six easy lessons? Or how to be happy though married?'

'If you're going to be funny . . . '

'But I'm not. I'm perfectly serious. Information on any of those subjects would be of unlimited value to you. Ah! Here're the eggs. Join me, Inspector?'

'Well . . . ' said Sharkey, weakening as his mouth began watering.

In two minutes egg was disappearing down his capacious gullet like money into the Tote at the dog track on a Saturday afternoon. For the space of four eggs he paused only to grasp salt or pepper and slices of toast. And having slowed down a little, he heaved a sigh of relief and toyed idly with his fifth egg.

Denby smiled and said, 'Only four. Aren't you hungry today, Inspector?'

Sharkey said, 'Matter of fact I haven't had any breakfast. Been on the devil of a stiff case — that's why I'm here now. I think perhaps you can help.'

The young writer poured the coffee and slid a cup over to Sharkey. The maid came to clear away the dishes. Sharkey glanced at her with appreciation as she bent over the table, flashing silk-clad legs, and said, 'You certainly know how to pick your harem. How on earth do you get maids like *that*? We never seem to have a pretty maid at home. They all wear black woollen stockings and have their hair in a bun.'

'You're married,' pointed out Denby reasonably. 'I'm not. I pick them myself. The girl who showed you in is my secretary, Miss Volt. But what's on the thing you call a mind, Inspector?'

'Have you read your morning paper?'

'I have.'

'You've seen the splash about the case of murder at the Elite Splenda last night?'

'Murder?' said Denby, raising his brows. 'But I understood that it couldn't have been murder. They say no one was near enough to have strangled the man.'

Sharkey snorted, 'I know. But you can't damn well get away from those marks on his neck, can you? They're there all right. I did wonder if he'd been poisoned by some drug which gives the effect of strangulation, but he hadn't. Besides, there were decided finger marks on the neck.'

'Then you haven't a single clue as to

how the killing was effected?'

'Not even as much as a hair.'

'But what can I do to help you?' asked Denby interestedly.

Sharkey looked a little embarrassed but said, 'That's what I'm here to find out. You know a lot about the supernatural, black magic, witch-doctor stuff. I read your last book. Now there was a suggestion that this was a supernatural death. I wondered if you remembered any parallel case in your researches?'

Denby laughed and said, 'There have been one or two, but all have admitted of natural explanations. Remember, Inspector, I spend my time disproving the supernatural and the occult. I do not believe in it. So how *could* I help you?'

'By doing just what you make a living doing, and proving this is not a murder through supernatural causes. At present that seems to be the only answer — but I feel certain, personally, there's more to it than meets the eye. Will you help, Collins?'

Denby Collins looked thoughtfully at the coffee grounds in the bottom of his cup, then said, 'Have you tried working on the case from another angle? Suppose you forget about how it was done, and find out *why* it was done first. That may give you some clue, if you find a strong enough motive.'

'Then you definitely don't believe it was the work of . . . well, of — forces alien to this life?'

Denby chuckled and poured more coffee. He said, 'I certainly do not. Every happening must have a perfectly natural explanation. Suppose you try the motive angle?'

'That's no use — we don't have to go far to find a motive for the murder of Caleni Ventura. There must be about a hundred or so people in London alone who hated him enough to kill him.'

'Hmm. He wasn't a popular character then?'

'About as popular as a South American skunk — which, speaking confidentially, was exactly what he was. Also confidentially, we aren't too sorry to be rid of him; he caused us quite a lot of trouble one way or another. But then again, justice must be done, and it doesn't matter what a man's like; if he gets killed it's our job to find the murderer.'

'Could I take a look at the body?' suggested Denby. 'It will be in the mortuary, I take it?'

'Yes, it's in the morgue. Caleni hadn't any relations — or any friends for that matter. When would you like to see it?'

'Now!'

Sharkey went a little pale and caressed his corpulent stomach. 'N — now?' he stuttered. 'After — after just eating *eggs*?'

'What the devil have eggs to do with it? You must learn to look at these things in a detached sort of way, Sharkey. In, as it were, the abstract. Although,' he went on doubtfully, eyeing the stout inspector's frontal contours, 'I suppose nothing about you could be absolutely abstract, not even thoughts. You're far too corporeal. But be that as it may, it's now or never, Inspector. All right?'

Sharkey said, 'I suppose so,' and waited until Denby had changed into his morning suit. Then, leading the way, still looking tremendously unenthusiastic, he escorted Denby Collins to the police car which was waiting.

As they turned out of the apartment, a young, pretty girl turned in, and Denby stopped abruptly. Sharkey grunted, 'What are you waiting for?'

'That girl — she must want to see me — can't disappoint her. Be back in a tick, Inspector.'

He hurriedly turned and followed the girl in, catching her up as she stood undecidedly in the sitting room, looking about her. As he tapped her on the shoulder, she started and gave a little gasp: 'Oh!'

'Sorry I startled you,' said Denby, smiling. 'But I was just leaving. I assume you were calling on me?'

'Why, er, are you Mr. Collins?'

'The same.'

'The author of *Spirits Are the Bunk*?'

'Still the same,' agreed Denby, gratified that she should know his work.

The girl gripped his arm and said, 'Oh, Mr. Collins, I need your help — badly. I hate to intrude on you . . .'

'Not at all. I like it. Intrude any time you feel that way. But I really can't stay right now. I've just committed myself to a most boring morning with a Scotland Yard gentleman who carries some weight, both literally and figuratively. I won't be too long if you'd care to wait. Or is it terribly urgent?'

She looked disappointed but said, 'No, not terribly. Perhaps, if it wouldn't be too much trouble, you could call on me at my home? I'm sure what I have to say would interest you from the point of view of your literary works.'

Denby said, 'I'm intrigued. Just leave the address with my secretary and I'll squeeze you in some corner — or perhaps I should say I'll try to fit you in.' He smiled at her, noting the small nose, the inviting lips, the blue eyes which looked as if they had contained tears shortly before.

She nodded and said, 'You've no idea how worried I am. You will come, won't you?'

Denby said, 'Rely on it. I've always wanted to help a damsel in distress. I wouldn't miss the opportunity for worlds. More so since you happen to be a particularly good-looking damsel. If you'll give me the address . . . ?' She handed him a tiny visiting card and he stowed it in his wallet. He said, 'Goodbye for now, Miss Calthorp. I'll be round the moment I've finished with Inspector Sharkey.'

There was a sudden bull-like roar from the doorway. 'Are you coming, Collins? What the devil . . . ?'

'Rather resembles a bull elephant calling to its young, doesn't it?' said Denby to the girl. 'But it isn't, you know; only Sharkey getting impatient. He got that voice when he was a humble 'copper' telling people to move along.'

And with a last pleasant nod to the girl, he was gone.

★   ★   ★

Denby Collins stood up and Sharkey, looking slightly unsettled, drew the sheet over the cadaver. 'Bit of a mess, isn't it?'

'It is, rather,' agreed Denby. 'But I'd be willing to swear it wasn't done by any supernatural agency. Yet . . . '

'Exactly what I say. Can we believe all

those people were too blind to notice anyone actually strangling him? If anyone was there, they *must* have spotted it. Yet . . . they didn't.'

'I once saw an interesting thing in India,' observed Denby. 'A yogi was ostensibly buried alive for fifteen weeks in the presence of twenty people. The same twenty saw him dug up fifteen weeks later. But he was *never* buried — I debunked that in my last book. The spectators were mass-hypnotised. Now, if the dancers could have been hypnotised in the same way . . . '

'But they couldn't. It wouldn't be credible.'

'I suppose not.' On their way out the morgue keeper called Sharkey to the telephone, saying the Yard wanted him. The inspector listened in silence for a moment, then said, 'I'll be right over to see him.' Turning to Denby he said, 'That was Sir Aram Carper — he just reported that his life has been threatened over the phone!'

3

The Terror Strikes Again!

Denby Collins decided to gravitate with the chief inspector towards the suburban home of Sir Aram Carper. He was interested, for Sir Aram was quite a big noise in the city. And since Sharkey didn't seem to resent his presence, he stuck close.

They alighted at the home of the threatened gentleman, walked up the drive to the door, and knocked. The door was opened almost immediately — furtively at first; and then, as Sharkey flashed his credentials, it swung wide and they were admitted by a thin, emaciated-looking young man wearing horn-rimmed spectacles and a worried expression.

'Inspector,' he said thankfully. 'I'm so glad you've come. I've been half out of my wits to know what to do for the best.'

'How's that?' Sharkey asked. 'Who're you?'

'I am Sir Aram's private secretary — my name is Alan Briggs. I was with Sir Aram when he received the telephone message. He's been suffering rather badly from gout lately, and has been confined to his bed. About an hour ago he had this telephone call in his room, and it really gave him a shaking up. The — the voice was that of a man, and it simply said, 'You have seen what I did to Señor Ventura, your fellow swindler — prepare yourself for your own death at any moment'!'

'Fellow swindler?' asked Denby sharply. 'Had Sir Aram any connections with the man who was killed last night?'

'Señor Ventura? Yes indeed, sir. He was a member of the board of directors of Señor Ventura's firm Public Promotions, and was also one of the chief shareholders.'

'I see. Go on.'

'Then, after these words, the phone went dead. Sir Aram was, not unnaturally, somewhat upset by the threat. He at once got in touch with Scotland Yard and asked for Chief Inspector Sharkey, whom the newspapers say is handling the case. They gave him a phone number to try — and he located you there.'

'You are sure the voice on the phone mentioned Señor Ventura? And you are equally sure it said prepare yourself for death at *any* moment?'

'Absolutely sure, Inspector. Sir Aram repeated the message to me immediately, and asked my advice and help.'

'Did he say what kind of voice it was?'

'He said only that it sounded like the voice of a maniac.'

'And what steps did you take for his protection until we arrived?'

'I stayed with him until I heard your taxi outside. Then I came to let you in, locking his bedroom door behind me.'

'I see. May we go up and see him at once?'

The secretary nodded, turned, and led the way upstairs. They walked along a short corridor to a room with large double doors.

Sharkey said, as the secretary fitted his key, 'By the way, are there no servants here?'

Briggs shook his head and replied, 'Not

this morning, Inspector. Sir Aram gave them permission to attend the Servants' Ball at the Weylands' home out of town. They are staying the night and returning this afternoon.'

'Then you and Sir Aram are alone here?'

He nodded, opened the door, and said, 'Chief Inspector Sharkey, sir.' The inspector walked in, followed by Denby Collins.

The appointments of the room were excellent; comfortable to the point of luxury. Shaded lamps hung from a high ceiling; there was morocco-bound furniture, thick lambs'-wool rugs, and a number of interesting antiques in the form of scimitars, swords, Indian kris, long-handled daggers, and various types of battle-axes. The long windows shed a sheet of daylight onto the high, canopied bed — and at that point the whole effect of the room was ruined by the ugly reality which lay there!

It was a man, obviously Sir Aram; his snowy beard, in places, was dyed a deep, glistening red colour; his features were screwed up in horror; the bedclothes over his chest were sodden wet with blood from the smiling gash across his scrawny throat. His right arm was thrown up across his eyes, as if to ward off some nightmare terror.

He was extremely dead.

The secretary reeled against the door-jamb with a smothered cry.

Sharkey said, 'Damn it to hell!' Denby Collins walked over and stood looking down at the curved scimitar which lay on the foot of the bedding; at the grim redness of the blade.

The secretary shuddered. 'But it's impossible! I swear no one was in this room when I left, and the only key to this door is the one I have.'

Sharkey touched the body and said, 'He can't have been dead more than a few minutes. Must have been murdered either just before, or since, we came.'

'I — I can't believe it,' muttered Briggs. 'I — I'd only left him about two minutes before I admitted you gentlemen! And not only that, but no one could have got into the house at all. All doors were locked and bolted!'

'You didn't hear any screams?'

'No — but I wouldn't have, anyway. This room is practically soundproof when the door is locked. The walls are extremely thick, and the door fits perfectly.'

Sharkey picked up the phone and gave his number. He got through and said, 'Wilson? Yes, Sharkey. Send a van over to take another corpse away. Round up the photographer, fingerprint man, and two plain clothes men. Send the divisional surgeon with them to Sir Aram Carper's home. Yes, he's been killed. Hurry that up.' He slammed down the phone, turned back to Briggs and said, 'I'll have to take you in, Briggs.'

Briggs nodded dully. He said, 'I knew you would, of course. But you don't really believe . . . ?'

'Frankly, I don't know what to believe. But you needn't worry — if you haven't done it we'll find out. What do you think about it, Collins?'

Denby Collins shrugged his shoulders and said, 'It seems fairly clear to me that it wasn't Briggs at all. How about the phone call? Briggs was in the room with

Sir Aram, wasn't he?'

'Yes. But how do we know it wasn't a ruse? How do we know he was definitely in the room at that time? It might all have been arranged to throw us off the scent.'

'That's possible — but there's another thing to be considered. In my humble opinion, this case is connected with the Ventura killing. Both men were directors on the board of Public Promotions. It's far too big a coincidence *to be a coincidence*. I believe, in view of the phone call, that whoever killed Ventura killed Carper. And if Briggs has an alibi for last night, it couldn't have been him.'

'I have, sir,' said Briggs eagerly. 'I was with Sir Aram all night.'

'That isn't much good,' Sharkey said irritably, 'since Sir Aram can't verify it. Did any of the servants see you?'

'I — why, no. They all left early to attend this ball I spoke of.'

'You see,' Sharkey, explained, 'we have to look at every angle of a case like this. Now if you'd had a *motive* for murdering Sir Aram Carper, you might have seized the opportunity afforded by the killing of

33

Ventura. You could have put through a phone call from downstairs, pretending to be your employer. Then you could have slipped upstairs, murdered him, locked the door, and come down to let us in. It would have been that simple. You would have counted on us thinking it was yet another inexplicable crime like last night's affair. But if there's a motive unearthed which proves it would have been *in your interests* to kill Sir Aram, things'll look pretty bad for you, Briggs.'

Briggs gave a resigned sigh and said, 'In that case they *do* look black. I may as well tell you myself — you'd find it out sooner or later anyway: Sir Aram was attached to me, having no family or intimate friends. In his will he left me the whole of his estate.'

★   ★   ★

Denby Collins eased his car into the drive of a small house, standing in its own grounds, in the outer suburbs. It was a bungalow type of structure, with mullioned windows and rustic cross pieces

34

running over a white, dapple-stoned façade. The garden was well cared for; and the perfume of roses wafted to Denby's nostrils, reminding him inexplicably of the girl he had come to see. He would have expected her to have lived in a home like that; it was just the exact place to be in keeping with her looks. He recalled the brief glimpse he had had of her: tawny-gold hair, full red lips, wide blue eyes, nose slightly retroussé, clothing fashionable and neat without ostentation.

He climbed from the car and walked towards the door and was about to knock, when the sound of sobbing stopped his hand in mid-air. It came from a window to the right and, treading cautiously over the lawn, he applied his eye to the crack where it had been slightly opened to let in air.

The girl he had met at his office was there, sitting in a deep armchair, face buried in her hands, shoulders shaking convulsively. Denby felt a twinge of pity for her and returned to the door. He raised the knocker and knocked gently.

It was several minutes before she came;

when she did open the door he noticed that she had hastily wiped her tears away, smudging her mascara in the process. She gave him a forced little smile and said, 'I'm so awfully glad you came, Mr. Collins. Please do come in.'

He went in, pretending not to notice her tear-stained cheeks. She escorted him into the sitting room and indicated a chair. She said, 'I know you must be cursing me for being an awful nuisance . . . '

'Not at all. If you think I can be of any service I'm only too delighted.'

'I don't know whether you can or not yet, Mr. Collins. I've read all your books, and you seem to be able to explain away any happening that seems supernatural in any way. If only you could ease my mind about my father . . . '

'Father?'

'Yes; he and I live here together. We aren't very rich, but we have been happy. I couldn't wish for a kinder man than my father, and he seems perfectly content with my company — or, I should say, did so, until . . . until the night before last.'

'He's changed?'

'Not changed — *vanished*, Mr. Collins. Vanished entirely!'

Denby Collins said slowly, 'Please don't distress yourself, Miss Calthorp. Sit down, and tell me calmly and easily just what took place.'

She smiled bravely and sat down beside him on the settee. She wiped away a tear from under her eye with the tip of her index finger and sniffed. 'I don't know where to start, really. I know he's been working on something big for about three years now. You see, my father's a research chemist employed by Public Promotions, the manufacturing firm . . . '

'That's rather interesting — please go on.'

'He was experimenting on dyes for them, trying to discover new shades. Then suddenly he told me he was onto something big, and started continuing his experiments at night when he got home. He still seemed normal, just a little tired and overworked.

'The night before last, when he returned from work, he was abnormally

37

excited about something. He ignored the dinner I had ready for him, dashed right off upstairs and locked himself in his laboratory. I sat here reading, with the door open in case he called me for anything. For a long time I heard him moving about, then all the sounds stopped. He was silent then, until the clock struck ten. I thought perhaps he'd exhausted himself and had gone to bed. I made coffee and sandwiches and took them up to him . . . '

She broke off and said, 'You're going to think I'm insane when I tell you what I found, but it's perfectly true. I found the door of his lab open, the lights still on. The phials of chemicals he'd used for his experiments were handy. A large tin bowl, which had evidently contained some liquid, lay on the bench. And the small electric oven which he uses for drying the things he dyes was still switched on. But of my father there was no sign whatsoever!

'I'm afraid I panicked then; I called his name, ran all over the house looking for him, even went into the garden and road.

But he had gone completely, and it isn't like him to leave the house without telling me where he was going and when he'd be back. Besides which, as I said, I was sitting here with the door open, and if he'd come downstairs I would hardly have missed seeing him.

'I communicated with the police and said he'd vanished. I told them why I was so worried, but they didn't place much credence in my story. They sent a constable round for particulars, which I gave him, and he came to the conclusion that Father had left the house suffering from amnesia, and was wandering about somewhere trying to recall who he was. He assured me they'd find him in time, and told me not to worry. But I *am* worried, Mr. Collins. I can't help it — nor can I believe Father was suffering from amnesia or anything else. I still say, why did he leave the light and oven on? Why didn't I see him going downstairs? Why was he so excited that night?' She concluded and sat silently, her fists clenched.

Then she said, 'That's why I came to you, Mr. Collins. I can't help being afraid there may be something . . . abnormal in his disappearance; something supernatural. If you can prove to me there isn't, I'll feel much more at ease. But perhaps you think as the policeman did — perhaps you think I'm exciting myself without cause, and he'll turn up in good time of his own accord?'

Denby stood up and took her hand. He said, 'I don't, Miss Calthorp. I think you're a particularly level-headed young lady, and not at all dumb. If you say you didn't see your father creep past you down the stairs, I confidently believe you didn't. And I'll do all that's in my power to help you. First of all, have you any objection to my inspecting his laboratory?'

'None at all. It's exactly as he left it — or, rather, as it was when he . . . he vanished.'

She led him up a small flight of stairs, cautioning him to duck the low rafters above his head. The laboratory was the only room to which stairs led; it was constructed over the kitchen of the single-story bungalow, and was small and hardly six feet high, but contained a great deal of equipment. Apparently it had been built in as an afterthought when the house had been constructed, for just such a use as Calthorp had put it to.

Denby inspected the tin bowl and the oven, then wandered round idly reading the names on the various test tubes and bottles. He turned to the girl at last and said, 'I have a pretty good knowledge of chemistry, but I'm afraid some of these names are Dutch to me. For instance, what on earth is dehetytalatin?'

'Oh, I think that is perhaps one of Father's own compositions. He was, I know, preparing various formulae which were entirely new to chemistry.'

'You have no idea why he was particularly excited about the dyes he was working on?'

'I haven't, Mr. Collins. None.'

Denby picked up a small desk pad, gazing curiously at the signs and symbols thereon. He said, 'I have a friend who's rather more versed in these matters than I am. He understands these things. Have you any objection to my taking this pad?'

'Not if you think it will help.'

'I do. I'm inclined to believe that your father's strange disappearance has something to do with his work. I'll do the best I can to find out what — but please don't expect too much. If he returns in the meantime, I'll hand this formula back to him.'

He left soon afterwards, leaving the girl a little more settled in her mind.

* * *

Miss Volt flitted calmly into Denby's bedroom and shook him by the shoulder. She said, 'Wake up, lazybones. Here's some coffee for you. You've a lot of appointments today.'

He yawned, sipped the coffee, and picked up the morning paper she had brought in. He read: 'ANOTHER GRUESOME MURDER! THIRD MAN KILLED BY MYSTERIOUS MEANS! Late last night, while enjoying the final act of *Carmen* at the Opera House, James P. Beesly was brutally stabbed to death by unknown agents. Mr. Beesly was occupying a box with his wife and daughter, and was one minute quite well and cheerful, and the next slumped forward with a knife in his heart. Mr. Beesly is a director of Public Promotions, and the third to be killed within two days!'

4

You Can't Escape!

Chief Inspector Ebenezer Sebastian Sharkey (unkindly christened thus by unthinking parents) gazed morosely into his whisky glass, and finally set it down on the small table with a thump. He was worried; this was nothing unusual for Sharkey, since he invariably had two or three distinct crimes on hand, all requiring a solution at the same time. But this was different — these murders were, considered Sharkey, going beyond a joke!

He glanced through the evening newspapers again, where a full report of the stabbing at the Opera House was given. The report was lurid in the extreme, the journalist responsible for it having given it his best. The word 'unnatural' appeared six times in three newspapers, and at the end of each report appeared the wrath-inspiring information (to Sharkey at least) that the police were completely baffled.

It was true, of course; in this case Sharkey hadn't been able to even give the time-honoured formula of arrest expected shortly. He hadn't even been able to give them the customary 'the police are anxious to interview a dark man with a scar on forehead, wanted for questioning in connection with the crime'. He'd had to admit he was completely bewildered — and the reporters had made the most of it and given it full prominence.

Sharkey sighed again, and glanced about the lounge at the other members of the Curzon Crime Club who happened to be present. His gaze had barely returned to his glass when a cheerful hand smote him violently upon the back, and a merry voice said, 'Well, well, well, if it isn't Sharkey. Brace up, man, you look about ready to hand in your badge!'

Sharkey glared up, opening his mouth to deliver a few well-chosen sentences; then seeing who stood above him he relaxed again and said, 'Oh, hello, Collins. Tried to get you on the phone last night — wanted you to slip along and have a look at the scene of the crime. You weren't home, according to your secretary.'

'No, I wasn't, laddie. Had a date with a rather superior angel. But I'm here now, and if there's anything I can help you with, say the word. How did this killing happen?'

'How do any of them happen? Seems the man was all right one second; the next he fell forward with a damned long dagger driven through his back and right into his heart. Died instantaneously.'

'Phew! Who was with him besides wife and daughter?'

'That's the damnable part of it — no one. The three were entirely alone in the box, and the page boy outside swears not a soul passed him.'

'And the man was another of the directors of Public Promotions?'

'He was. That's three of them gone, and the other three have been ringing the Yard up all day, demanding to know what's being done about the murders. Believe me, I've been getting hell. But I can't understand it — how? Why? Who? Candidly I've never had such an awkward case, Collins. I confess I'm completely, er . . . '

'Go on, *say it*' said Denby with a grin. 'Everyone else has.'

'*Baffled*!' Sharkey said, wincing. 'Completely baffled. The Yard is competent to deal with any ordinary crime — and I'll guarantee not one murderer in a thousand would get away with three crimes like the three which have happened. But how the hell can anyone arrest or track down a killer who *isn't?* That's what I'd like to know.'

Collins nodded and said, 'I think you'll have to release Sir Aram's secretary now, won't you? Clearly this crime ties in with the other two, and if he was in jail he could hardly have committed this one.'

Sharkey nodded and grunted as he eased his immense girth up from the seat. He said, 'I've already released him, Collins. Got a plain clothes man on his tail just in case, but I never did believe it was him.'

Collins said, 'Sit down, Inspector, and have one with me. You aren't in any hurry, are you?'

'Not particularly. I was going over to see the other three directors of Public Promotions but I've time to spare for another drink, I suppose. Perhaps you'd like to come along with me?'

'What exactly are you calling on them for?'

'Mainly to see if they know anything which might account for their partners' deaths. And also to ask them if they feel in need of police protection. I feel sure we haven't had the last death in this series by a long way. There's a bee in my bonnet which buzzes the fact that whatever is happening to these directors *is going to happen to all of them.*'

They sat drinking whisky for some time, then Sharkey hauled himself up again and said, 'Coming?'

'I'm right with you, Inspector. This affair gets more and more fascinating every minute. Carry on.'

They left the club and took a taxi. Sharkey gave the address as the Strand Hotel, explaining to Collins that Millicent, one of the three remaining directors, maintained bachelor apartments there.

They found Millicent surrounded by an array of shirts, socks and ties, hastily packing with the help of his valet, Arnolds. Arnolds opened the door cautiously to them and said, 'Who is calling, sir?'

'Chief Inspector Sharkey of Scotland Yard. I should like a word with Mr. Millicent.'

Millicent called, 'Show him in, Arnolds.'

They went in and Millicent didn't even stop his packing for introductions. He said, 'I can spare you only a few minutes. If you have anything to ask me, please go ahead and ask.'

He was stringy and slightly grey on the temples. His lips were thin and cruel-looking, mere gashes in his taut flesh. There was a germ of panic lurking behind his apparently unflustered gaze.

Sharkey said, 'It's about your partners — your fellow directors. I wondered if you knew of any reason why anyone would murder them?'

'I know of plenty — but what good would they be to you if I told you?'

'Oh, I admit the murderer hasn't been

49

seen — but if we could get at a *motive* for their deaths . . . '

Millicent stopped packing and faced the inspector. He said, 'Have you any idea of how this series of murders is being committed?'

'We know *how* they're committed — what we don't know is by whom. If there is anyone you know of who might have the incentive, it's your duty to tell us.'

Millicent laughed harshly and said, 'Inspector, if I started telling you the people who have incentive to murder us directors of Public Promotions, I'd be here until midnight. And that wouldn't do, since I'm catching the eight-ten train . . . '

'You are? You're leaving London?'

'Wouldn't *you* leave London if you thought your life was in danger? No, I suppose you wouldn't — couldn't, being a policeman. But I happen to have a horror of murder — especially when it's quite likely to be my own.'

'Where are you going?'

'Never mind that. But wherever it is, it couldn't be any less safe than London right now. I'll tell you that it's out in the wilds of Scotland — a little retreat I've visited before. But that's all I'm saying.'

'You realise, of course, you're cutting yourself off from police protection?'

'Is that such a terrible loss? The police, as far as this case is concerned, seem to be completely — '

'Don't say it,' yapped Sharkey, holding up a protesting hand and going red in the face. 'Don't say *baffled*, for God's sake.'

'I was going to say completely at a loss, but perhaps 'baffled' is the better word after all. No, Inspector, I won't worry about cutting myself off from police protection one little bit.'

'How about these people you claim might have a motive for killing your friends?'

'Not my *friends*, Inspector, please. Business associates, if you don't mind. None of us were friends, I assure you. We stuck together because it paid us, and six brains scheme better than one. Oh, don't look so shocked. You know our records well enough. We've always kept within the law, but only just.'

'Now you mention it, I agree,' said

Sharkey. 'You can keep within the law and still break the laws of common humanity. I think you and your frie — business associates have done that repeatedly.'

'We have,' said Millicent with a faint sneer. 'In fact, if you look at it from one angle we all deserve to die. But I have no intention of staying to receive my unwelcome reward for my rotten life. I'm going where this damned thing, whatever it is, can't strike me.'

'It seems to me it can strike you wherever you go,' Sharkey told him. 'If it can strike silently, unseen, it can surely find you no matter how far away you are.'

'I doubt it. Let me tell you at once that I feel certain there's some human agency behind the murders. And I'm perfectly willing to bet no human agency could ever find me where I propose to spend the next few months — or even years, if necessary.'

He had hardly finished speaking when the telephone rang. Over the wire, when he picked it up, came a thin, clear voice; it was precise, mechanical, like the voice of some automaton set to say certain words at a certain time. It was devoid of any cadence, and reminded Denby Collins of a remorseless judge delivering a death sentence. The words rang clear across the room, causing everyone present to stiffen.

'Am I speaking to Mr. Vincent Millicent?'

'Yes, yes, you are. What is it?'

'I am aware you are packing. I know you plan to leave London. May I remind you that you might just as well stay? You are the next — *and you can't escape!*'

Millicent's face went ashy grey; his fingers relaxed and the phone clattered against the table, then dangled upon the end of its cord. Sharkey recovered first and dashed across to the phone — if it is possible for a man of Sharkey's dimensions to be described as having dashed; lumbered, perhaps, would be the better word — picked it up, and said, 'Hello — *hello*! Are you there?' There was no answer. Sharkey tinkled the phone rest and said, 'Operator? This is a police call. Get me the number of the person who just phoned these apartments.'

He waited a moment; then his face fell.

He said, 'But surely . . . Are you absolutely certain?' He replaced the receiver on its hook and said, 'That call didn't go through the exchange. It must have been a house call. Wait a minute . . . ' He picked the phone up again and said, 'Is that the desk? Good. Someone just put through a call to four-forty. Can you tell me from which apartment the call came?' He slapped down the phone again and said, 'Came from one of the booths in the lobby. Hang on here — I'm going down there.'

When he had gone, Millicent poured a glass of whisky with a shaking hand and offered one to Denby Collins, who accepted. Arnolds, the valet, suddenly said, 'If you'll excuse me, sir, I'd prefer not to come along on this trip with you. I — '

'What?' Millicent's hand shook, and the whisky he held spilled. He said hoarsely, 'I'm relying on you, man. Damn it, you can't let me down now like this.'

'I'm sorry, sir. I'd prefer to remain here.'

'You can't think it will be safe, eh, is that it? Well, you're coming, you spineless fool. I'm the one in danger, not you. Or do you think we both might be finished off?'

'I think it quite likely, sir; and if you insist on my presence, I'm afraid I must ask you to accept my resignation.'

'*Done* — but you've still a month's notice to work, Arnolds. Don't forget that. So you're still coming along.'

'I'm sorry, sir, but I must ask you to release me at once. If you refuse to do so, I shall refuse to accompany you — I will not work the month's notice.'

Millicent's eyes narrowed into two slits. He said, 'Arnolds, if you walk out on me now, like this, I'll take damn good care you don't get a job as valet anywhere else! I'll have you blacklisted at the agencies.'

'Then I'll have to make the best of that, sir. Whatever you choose to do, I mean to leave. I'm sorry it had to happen this way.'

'You mean to say you're afraid because of that tomfool phone call?'

'No. It was my intention to leave anyway, but I hesitated to speak before.'

Millicent cursed and mopped down

more whisky. The spirit was giving him fresh courage; his eyes were brighter. He said, 'Leave then, and be damned to you. I'll get along just as well without an old woman attached to me. But if you imagine for one minute that you're going to get your last month's salary, you're mistaken!'

Arnolds turned away calmly and continued with the packing. The bags were fastened and strapped when Sharkey returned, and at the expression on his features, Denby had a hard struggle to control his mirth. Never had he seen anything half so lugubrious as Sharkey's face. It was a study in blank bewilderment.

Denby chuckled. 'Good God, Inspector — don't tell me the police are *completely baffled* again?'

Sharkey snorted. 'They are. How could they help it? Who isn't baffled? Why should the police be singled out for derision?'

'Mainly because it happens to be their job to solve things like this. But tell us — what happened? Did you find the phone booth?'

'Yes, I found it. I also found a desk

clerk who swore no one had used it within the last half hour. He was certain of that. Now what?'

Millicent said, 'The operator on the house connections must have been mistaken about the call coming from that booth.'

'No. I went round and asked her. She swore it had come from the booth she had told me. She may have been mistaken, and tried to cover herself up by insisting she was right — quite a lot of people do. We'd be spared a good many headaches at the Yard if only people would keep their mouths shut until they're certain what they mean to say is right in every detail. But they don't. They state a thing definitely, and after we've been to a hell of a lot of trouble to enquire into their statements, they begin humming and hawing and saying 'I could have *sworn* I was right'.'

Millicent drank more whisky and said, 'Are we here for a discussion on the psychology of witnesses? If so, I hope you gentlemen will excuse me.'

Sharkey said, 'So you're still going?'

'After that phone call, more than ever. I'd like you two gentlemen to see me to the station if you don't object. My man has turned out to be a yellow-livered skunk.' He directed a scornful glare at the back of Arnolds, who stiffened but ignored the remark.

'We'll see you down there,' agreed Sharkey. 'Is that all right by you, Collins?'

'Certainly. I'm very interested in this case and very grateful to you, Inspector, for allowing me to follow it up so closely.'

Millicent said, 'I — aren't you a policeman?'

'Do I look like one?'

'Well, now you mention it, no. You haven't the flat feet or the traditional Derby — nor have you that overfed look.'

Sharkey grunted murderously and said, 'Are we going, or are we having an informal discussion on the physical handicaps of the members of the force?'

Some of Millicent's nervousness returned as he walked down to the cab with them at either side. His eyes shot furtively to right and left; his under lip trembled visibly. They gained the taxi without mishap, and were swiftly transported to the station. It was crowded with night travellers, and Sharkey and Collins watched the fugitive while he purchased his ticket, then walked along to the platform with him. For some minutes they stood listening to the hollow, eerie echoes which rang across the vast depot; then the piercing shrill of escaping steam made Sharkey jump, and the train began to pull out.

Millicent leaned from the window and shouted, 'Thanks for the bodyguard — I'll be quite safe now . . . '

Two sharp cracks came from immediately behind Sharkey; and two neat, round holes appeared in Millicent's forehead. He slumped back from the window, into the carriage, as life left him . . .

5

Crazier and Crazier

It could only have been a matter of seconds after those shots had shattered the air under the massive station dome, before several things happened all together.

First, Denby Collins jumped for the moving train, tore open a door, tumbled into the carriage and automatically reached up for the communication cord, which the railway authorities are sporting enough to let one pull for five pounds a throw.

Secondly, Chief Inspector Sharkey — with a speed surprising for a man of his bulk — whirled round like a spinning dervish, and got hold of the lapels of the coat belonging to the only person in his immediate vicinity.

Thirdly, the train squealed to a full stop before it had moved more than five yards. Denby Collins came out of the compartment again and sprinted along the train, looking in at the windows. Millicent had had a first to himself — and he still had. He was sprawled ungraciously on the floor, taking up seats with his feet. He had clearly been kneeling on the seat looking from the window when the slugs had perforated him. He had fallen backwards, feet remaining in place and head cannoning into the gangway.

It only took Denby a moment to ascertain that he wouldn't be home to dinner. He got out of the compartment again and dusted his suit as Sharkey came panting up, still gripping his captive. The captive was none other than the valet, Arnolds, wearing a slightly bewildered expression under his black Homburg hat.

Sharkey said, 'He's dead?'

'They don't come any deader,' said Denby grimly. 'He found out what he was told on the phone . . . you can't escape.'

Sharkey said, 'Look who I found right behind me! What would you make of that?'

Denby looked at the valet, who said, 'I — I don't understand why you're pulling me about.'

'You trying to say you know nothing about this?' grunted Sharkey, quelling the wave of travellers and guards and engine stokers who were clustering round, with a flash of his police badge.

'No, I don't. I heard the shots. I admit they seemed to come from right beside me. But I certainly never fired them.'

'We left you back at the hotel. You and the dead man in that carriage had a quarrel with each other, isn't that so? Okay, how come you're down here now, on the spot at his murder?'

Arnolds glanced round frantically and said, 'I know how it looks. I know the truth is going to sound silly, but I'll tell you. I was fond of Mister Millicent. He was nasty at times, but on the whole we got on well together, and he treated me decently. I felt guilty about letting him down when he seemed to need me so much, and I couldn't resist coming along myself to see him off.'

'You expect us to believe that?'

'It doesn't matter whether you do or not. It's the truth, and my conscience is clear.'

'Then what's this?' growled Sharkey, who had been hastily searching the suspect. He dragged from the man's jacket pocket a Colt automatic. 'Is this yours?'

Arnolds looked amazed. He said, 'Why, yes, I admit it is. I only bought it this morning on Mister Millicent's orders; he said I'd better be prepared to help him if anything unpleasant happened to him, as it had to his fellow directors. But — I could have taken an oath that I left it back at the hotel!'

Sharkey said, 'You'll be taking an oath on this business all right — look at this!' He spun the chambers, extracting five bullets and one expended case. He said, 'Here — smell the gun.'

Arnolds, face blank, sniffed. Sharkey said, 'No need to tell you that gun's been fired within the last five minutes, is there? No need to tell you what goes if ballistics find out this gun fired the bullets in Millicent's body.'

'But I didn't. I don't know how that gun got in my pocket. I didn't even have it loaded. The — the bullets were lying in the drawer beside the gun. You've got to believe that, Inspector.'

'It isn't my job to believe anything. If you didn't do it you'll be all right. But I have to take you in just the same. The weight of evidence is too strong against you. Understand?'

Denby Collins said, 'Sure you aren't making another mistake? Remember the last time you took a man in — Briggs, wasn't it?'

'I know, I know. My memory's every bit as good as yours, Collins. And I wouldn't be surprised if I didn't have to release this man within a couple of days. But until something crops up to explain that gun in his possession, I'm holding him. Now suppose you look after him while I go and phone the Yard — I don't know why we damn well pay half the constables round here. Could you imagine — a murder committed in the busiest portion of the city, and there isn't even one policeman in sight.' And rumbling with irrepressible wrath, the rotund inspector departed to the nearest phone booth.

The valet said, his eyes darting with panic, 'Listen, sir. I didn't do it, honestly.

I thought too much of the master to ever do anything like that. You do believe me, don't you?'

'I believe you, Arnolds, yes. I'm sure Sharkey knows you're innocent too — but he has to do something.'

'But — but you'll tell them I didn't — '

'I'm sorry, I can't do anything on your behalf. I'm not a police officer. Just a second-rate writer, that's all. But take it easy. I guarantee within two days he'll *have* to let you out. I feel pretty sure that whoever's killing off the directors of Public Promotions will not neglect the remaining two members for very long.'

The valet nodded. Then, in sudden doubt, he said, 'Suppose — suppose the others aren't killed? Suppose — nothing else happens. I'll be tried and — and hung.'

'Hanged,' corrected Denby, lighting a cigarette and handing one to the valet. 'No, I don't think that will happen.'

'But it might — it might. Innocent men have been hung — hanged, before, haven't they? It could happen again, couldn't it?'

'It could — but I think you'll find it won't. I'm not pretending to know how it was worked, but perhaps the fingerprints on the gun will straighten things out for you. If you didn't fire it, your prints can't be on it.'

'But they can. I handled it last, and if whoever did fire it wore a glove, it would not leave his prints — only mine.'

Sharkey came back and said, 'All right. We wait for the Maria. Won't be long.'

The Black Maria rolled up within ten minutes and Arnolds, shivering with uncontrollable fear, was led to it. He hung his head as he passed through the crowd of gaping sightseers which surrounded the van, and through whom the police had to push their way.

The van rolled away, leaving Sharkey and Denby waiting for the other van — the van from the morgue.

★   ★   ★

Denby Collins turned in at the gates of a fashionable house in Berkeley Square, strummed a serenade on the knocker, and

66

smiled at the plump butler who opened the door to him.

'Morning, Chester,' he said lightly. 'How's the corpulency coming along?'

'Oh, perfectly, sir. Those tablets certainly help a lot. I've put on three inches round the waist since you recommended them to me. Thank you very much, sir.'

'Don't mention it, Chester,' said Denby, grinning. 'We don't want you wasting away to a shadow, do we?'

The butler glanced down with justifiable pride at his large avoirdupois, and shook his head. Chester was a man whose whole heart was sunk in his work — he loved his job. He was the perfect butler, and took a pride being such. And, in Chester's opinion, the perfect butler *had* to have a large stomach — it was an essential. Unless a man boasted a waistline like an inflated elephant, and a row of double chins, he didn't rank for a place even, in Chester's opinion.

The fatter the stomach the better the butler. So Chester was firmly convinced. And Denby, who had known the old retainer as long as he had known Professor Sylvester, the owner of the house, was aware of this belief of the butler's, and had presented him with some miraculous pills which guaranteed to put three inches on any and every portion of man's, or woman's, anatomy in less than three months. And with Chester they had worked!

'You desire to see the professor, sir?' said Chester, holding his feet duck-like and his elbows askew — another indispensable trait to Chester's idea of the perfect butler.

'That was the idea. Is he handy?'

'In the laboratory, sir.'

'Shoot me in, then,' Denby told him, and followed him through the hall, through the kitchens, and into the grounds at the rear of the house.

A small shed roofed with corrugated iron stood here, and as they approached their noses wrinkled, and Denby sniffed. He said, 'My God, Chester! Now what's he working on? It smells like burning socks.'

'I am not precisely aware of the nature of the master's experiment, sir, but I believe he is pursuing the creation of a new and exotic perfume.'

'Perfume? Great Scott, I'd have said he was trying to manufacture a patent manure! Have I got to trust my life in that gas chamber?'

Chester sniffed the foul air which emanated from the interior of the shed and remarked, as if he were savouring some new and delicate odour, 'Perhaps it is a trifle on the strong side, sir . . . '

'On the strong side? I'll say it is! You must be mistaken. This can't be perfume. Surely it's a new poison gas?'

'No sir; in spite of its present, er, unappetising flavour, I understand it is eventually to be a perfume which will retail at an astronomical price for a four-ounce bottle.'

'Really? What's he going to call it? Evening in a Parisian Sewer, or Glue Factory Special?'

The butler permitted himself the vestige of a smile; Mr. Collins was a humorous young gentleman. Denby went on, 'Really, Chester, I can't venture into that. My clothes would reek for weeks!'

'It isn't so bad when you get used to it,

69

sir,' explained Chester. 'One's nostrils become acclimatised to it. I doubt if the master would leave his experiment at this stage — you will have to brave it, sir.'

Denby said, 'Oh, well. Never let it be said I didn't risk a fate worse than death for a damsel in distress. Lead on, Chester.'

Chester led on, and they entered the lab. Professor Sylvester, his silvery head bent over a crucible above a Bunsen burner, his silvery beard entangled with the pipette with which he was stirring his foul smelling concoction, didn't even glance up.

Chester said, 'Hrrumph! Mr. Collins to see you, sir.'

'What? Eh? Collins — Denby Collins? Oh yes. Tell him I'm busy. Can't be disturbed. Tell him to go and play with his bogies and spirits and things.'

'But, sir . . . '

'Haven't you gone? Well, go now. Tell him I can't be disturbed!'

Denby grinned, stepped forward, and said, 'But you're going to be disturbed! I'm here, you old sinner! I heard every word you said. Is it nice to turn out an old friend when he's braved this foul stench to see you? Is it? I ask you.'

The professor glanced up and said, 'Well, well, my dear boy. I had no idea you were there, or I wouldn't have said what I did. Not that I didn't mean every word of it, mind, but one has to pander to the laws of etiquette, hasn't one? I'm so glad you dropped along to see me. How long are you staying?'

'Not very long, you old hypocrite.'

'Excellent, excellent. I'm engaged in a rather startling line of research — a perfume which has never been attempted before. Its characteristic odour will awaken every woman in the world!'

'I can well believe it,' grinned Denby. 'I'll be candid with you, you old humbug. I think you're making synthetic Gorgonzola!'

The old professor looked hurt. He said, 'Collins, just because I was your science teacher doesn't give you the right to hurl your gross insults at me. You have wounded me very deeply with your impertinent aspersions.'

'Well someone ought to stop you, Sylvester, before you obliterate mankind.'

'Would that be *such* a tragedy?' asked the professor keenly.

Denby chuckled, dug in his pocket, and produced the notebook he had taken from the lab of Calthorp's the night he had visited the girl. He laid it before Sylvester and said, 'There you are. Just give me all the dope you can on that and I'll leave you to your perfume.'

'Dope?'

'Information, then.'

Sylvester picked it up and gazed curiously at it; then he began flicking over the pages, nodding to himself every now and then. Denby waited patiently but the professor seemed to have forgotten his very presence.

Finally Sylvester said, 'Who did this belong to, Denby?'

'Man called Calthorp — research chemist for Public Promotions. Why, do you happen to know him?'

'I have a faint recollection of having read some of his articles in *Science Monthly*. I remember thinking at the time what a brilliant fellow he was.'

'He was? Hmm. I think he was onto something big the night he vanished — so his daughter told me.'

'Vanished? How do you mean, vanished?'

'Just that. Far as I can make out, he vanished cleanly and neatly without a trace.'

'You mean he's missing?'

'No. I mean vanished! At least, that's what his daughter claims.'

'But good God, my boy, men don't vanish just like that! It's fantastic.'

'So are these murders which are happening currently — but they're still happening. I have an idea his disappearance is tied up in some inexplicable way with the murders.'

'What makes you believe that?'

'Oh, it's only a hunch. There may be nothing at all in it. It's just that since all the victims of these murders are directors of Public Promotions, it seems funny to me that a man who is one of their most brilliant research chemists should vanish. I start wondering if he'd found out something, and what.'

'I think I see what you mean. And you hope that by these notes I'll be able to tell you the line he was working on?'

'Yes, I did hope that. The girl tells me he was experimenting will dyestuffs.'

The professor glanced at the notes and nodded. He said, 'At first glance there would appear to be a great many formulae here which would be of use to a man working on colours. But, this second page — what could this have to do with it?'

'What is it?'

'Mainly theorising about the reflection and refraction of light and colour rays. Spectra and polarisation of light. Technical stuff. When does that come in?'

Denby shrugged hopelessly and said, 'That's what I hoped you'd find out. Can you?'

'I expect I could discover the line he was following. It would take considerable time before I knew just what he was driving at. From a rough glance he might have been experimenting for any one of a dozen things.'

'I see. You'd have to work on it a while.

When could you let me know?'

'I'm not sure. Is it very urgent?'

'Very. I'd appreciate it a lot if you could let me have some dope — information — soon.'

'Well, all right, my boy. I suppose if the fellow's missing, the sooner we find out what he found out, the sooner we can get some idea of why he vanished. Unless, of course, his disappearance hadn't any connection with his work. Have you thought of that?'

'I have. But I believe it has a lot to do with his work.'

'Then I'll give these notes my attention tonight, and phone you the moment I've found out anything.' He stowed the notes in his pocket, picked up a phial of green liquid, and said, 'Now watch this — this will make all the difference to this per-fume!' He poured it in; Denby and Chester watched with interest. The potion bubbled. A nauseating, throat-searing smell arose, and with a gasp of 'Women and children first!', Denby broke out of the shed and left his friend to it!

6

Larsen Gets His Too

Manley Larsen took up the whisky glass with fingers that were a trifle unsteady, drained it, and looked again at Chief Inspector Sharkey. He said, 'So — so Millicent has — has been murdered?'

'He has. Last evening while leaving for Scotland. You must have read the report in the newspapers?'

'Yes, I have, Inspector. And it seems to me this killer is going to go on with his brutal murders. I demand protection — and by that I mean *effective* protection. Do you understand?' The man's eyes gleamed angrily at the inspector from beneath his bushy white brows; his yellowish features twitched nervously, and his left hand was pressed against the region of his heart.

Sharkey said, 'Don't excite yourself, Mr. Larsen.'

'Excite myself?' He rose up from his

chair, quivering with indignation. He pointed an accusing finger at the Yard man. 'I have a *right* to excite myself! Four murders have been committed in a fewer number of days — probably it will be my turn next. I know that's why you came to see me. Ventura, Sir Aram, Beesly and now Millicent. They were the four men who held the most shares in Public Promotions, in the order named. I hold the next largest block, so it's only natural to assume I will be the next victim. And you tell me not to excite myself!'

Sharkey sighed mournfully and plucked at the rim of his Derby hat. There was no denying it — Larsen certainly did have good cause for exciting himself.

Larsen went on, 'Unless you give me protection, Inspector, you'll be sorry. I happen to be a good friend of Assistant Commissioner Steele's, and I'll have that badge off your coat if anything happens to me.'

Sharkey forbore to ask him how he was going to manage that *after* something had happened to him — it promised to be a considerable feat. But he said, 'Don't worry. I have two men on guard here — back and front. No one will get past Kawker and Dixon.'

'They'd better not. I can't stand too much excitement — my heart isn't all it should be.'

Sharkey picked up his hat and said, 'I think I'll be going now. With Kawker and Dixon looking after the outside, and Moston on guard in the hall, nothing *could* happen to you.'

The telephone shrilled peremptorily across his remarks, causing Larsen to reel, almost. Stark terror showed in the director's eyes as he stared at the innocent-looking instrument. He said, 'Haven't — haven't two of the others — had *phone calls?*'

Sharkey said, 'Probably one of your friends. I'll take it.'

'No, no. It's all right — just wait . . . '

Larsen picked the phone up and stood with it clenched in his hand for a moment, trying to steel himself to take the call. Finally he brought it slowly, fascinatedly to his ear, as if it were some poisonous snake which was about to strike him. He said weakly, 'Man — Manley Larsen speaking.'

78

'Larsen? You're next — you know that, I suppose? You're next to go the way of those other damned thieving, swindling swine. Yours won't be a pleasant death, nor a sudden one. I have been looking forward to your elimination. If possible I detest your personal characteristics more than I did any of the others. It won't be long, Larsen. It won't be long . . . '

Larsen gave a hoarse cry, and the phone fell from his right hand. His left started to reach up for his heart, but never made it. He half-turned towards Sharkey, then his face contorted and he fell panting to the floor.

Sharkey jumped forward, lifted him on to the settee, and called for help. A maid and butler ran in; and the butler, having glanced at his master, at once picked up the phone and asked for a number. 'Is that Dr. Moss? Yes, Doctor, the master has had another bad attack. This is Vernam, his butler, speaking. Yes, it looks very bad to me. Expect you in ten minutes? Thank you, Doctor.'

Sharkey moved away from the director and picked up the phone. He said, 'Can you trace a call which came here about three minutes ago? Thank you.' He waited. A long wait. Then, 'Public call box? I see. Thank you.' He replaced the phone with a heavy groan, walked into the hall, and called, 'Moston!'

A plain clothes man hurried from the doorway. 'Yes, sir?'

'Get round the corner to Elm Tree Road. See if you can see anyone hanging about a call box there. That's all. If you see anyone who looks at all suspicious, bring him here.' Moston went, nodding. Sharkey returned to the other room and glanced down at the settee where Larsen lay, purple in the face and breathing hard. He said, 'Is he subject to these attacks?'

'Yes, sir,' Vernam told him. 'He has them regularly. Any little excitement sets him off. Only this is about the worst I've seen him. He won't be able to stand many like this.'

Sharkey thought to himself, *Perhaps the killer won't have to work on this one. Perhaps his voice and threat have done the job! Hmm. Save me a lot of trouble if the man passed out from a heart attack — I hope . . .*

He forced his uncharitable thoughts aside hurriedly. Larsen had begun to move feebly under the ministrations of maid and butler. He now sat with an effort, and regained some of his normal colour. He gasped, 'You heard that, Inspector? I told you — I told you I was next.'

'*I*'ve told *you* not to worry. No one can get in here — no one's going to do so. Forget it.'

'But who is this fiend? Who is it? Who could want to — to murder us off like a lot of cattle?'

'Don't you have any ideas? Your friend Millicent told me you'd all wronged so many people that hundreds must have a fair motive for killing you all off. Is that so?'

'Millicent talks too much. I know a lot of people have the feeling that — that we've — well, done them injustices. But there wasn't anything really unlawful. Their grudges are more fancied than actually incurred.'

'Can you name some of them for me?'

'Good heavens, no. I haven't a very good memory for names. But possibly Carson could tell you some possible suspects.'

'Carson? He's the other — and last — member of the board, is he not?'

'Yes. The least important. He holds only a small block of shares in the company.'

'Perhaps I'll call on him — after I've seen you safe.'

The doorbell rang, and the butler hastened to open the door. A tall, black-garbed man stood on the step. The butler said, 'Please come in, Dr. Moss. Mr. Larsen is in here, sir.'

The door closed behind the doctor, and the butler escorted him into the room where Sharkey and Larsen were. Dr. Moss set down his bag and walked over to his patient, saying, 'What's wrong now, old chap? Hear you've had a bad spell.'

'I have — my heart's still going like a trip-hammer.'

'Haven't I almost pleaded with you to take things calmly? I tell you, Mr. Larsen, I can't be responsible for what happens if you don't follow my orders implicitly and force yourself to take everything as a matter of course.'

Sharkey said, 'I don't think this could

be helped, Doctor. He had a telephone call from — well, from whoever or whatever has been murdering people recently.'

'Oh, I see. That upset you, old man, did it?'

Larsen nodded. He said, 'Doctor, this is Chief Inspector Sharkey of Scotland Yard. Inspector, this is Dr. Moss of Harley Street.'

'Pleased to meet you, Inspector,' said the doctor, smiling and shaking Sharkey's hand. 'I've read quite a great deal about your methods of capturing criminals; I feel sure you'll be successful in the present case, eventually.'

'I feel sure myself — but how eventually?' said Sharkey.

The doctor turned back to Larsen and said, 'Let me have your pulse.'

Larsen submitted to the examination, and when he opened his shirt for the stethoscope, the flesh above his heart was clearly visible pumping frantically up and down. Dr. Moss looked grave and said, 'You should be in bed. Your room's on the ground floor, isn't it?'

Larsen nodded and said, 'I feel terrible,

Doctor. My whole inside's turning over. Can you give me something?'

'I can give you a mild sedative, then we'll try and get you to your bed. Don't move for the moment.'

Larsen sat still whilst the doctor fumbled in his bag and brought out a small bottle. He measured off a portion into a beaker, placed it on the table and went to the door to call for a clean glass.

Larsen said, 'Doctor, what do you think of — of these murders?'

For a second Moss didn't reply; then he said, 'I'm a doctor of medicine, not a doctor of witchcraft. I advise you not to worry yourself, Mr. Larsen.' He returned to the table and poured the liquid from the beaker into the glass. He came over to Larsen and said, 'Here you are; drink this. It isn't too pleasant, but get it right down and it'll settle that pulsation you've got. Sharp's the word, now!'

Larsen tasted the fluid with a wry grimace and said, 'That's awful! Tastes worse than usual — bitter.'

'Imagination. Drink it up and you'll be all right. Hurry up.'

Larsen said, 'You're the doctor. Bottoms up.' He tilted the glass and drained the dose off rapidly.

Moss said, 'That's the idea. If I were you I'd give the whisky a miss for the time being. It doesn't help your condition.'

'I will if I live to be able to do so,' agreed Larsen fervently. 'Believe me, Doctor, I will . . . I . . . urr — urrr . . . '

Dr. Moss suddenly stiffened and stared; Sharkey came from the chair he was in, white-faced. Larsen's features had gone deathly pale — his jaw muscles had bound into tight knots bulging out of his cheeks. His lips were rigid. His breathing suddenly began to rasp from his throat in hard, tearing gushes . . . He started to his feet, eyes wild and frenzied, one hand darting down to the region of his stomach.

Then, while the other two gazed on spellbound, he hit the floor, rolled over, and arched his body in a taut semi-circle, forcing great sobbing gulps of air into his lungs. His body contracted, and they lifted him onto the settee again. A violent agony seemed to warp his body, and his back stiffened as he rose from the settee in an arch. His jaws were clenched as if he had been struck by a sudden attack of lockjaw, and fine specks of perspiration stood out on his features. He contorted sideways and fell to the floor; they picked him up again, and Sharkey said, 'For God's sake do something, Doc. Is this another heart attack?'

Moss said, 'No, no. I can't tell what's wrong with him, but — it looks to me as if he's been given one of the convulsive poisons!'

Now Larsen was thrashing about on the settee in an agony of torture, body arched spasmodically; and at each spasm his breath ceased to come and go entirely.

Dr. Moss rushed over to his bag and came back hastily with a selection of its contents. He said, 'I'll give him an anaesthetic to ease the contortions. It isn't really safe with his heart in that condition, but it will have to be done. If we can get him over these spasms without his suffocating, we'll have a chance. An emetic and sedative will fix him up then!'

He began to prepare the chloroform, while Larsen grew every minute more violent. It was plain that every nerve and fibre of the man's body was shrieking with blinding, intolerable torture. Moss bent down with the prepared nose pad — and suddenly Larsen's convulsions stopped, and he lay still and silent. A thin bluish-grey line began to be visible above his upper lip.

Sharkey said, 'What . . . ?'

Moss bent over the man; his face, when he rose, was grave. He said, 'The man's *dead*. His heart gave out.'

★ ★ ★

'So that was it,' said Sharkey, imbibing his fourth whisky at Denby Collins's apartments the following day.

'You say the glass he drank from was analysed? The dregs were full of strychnine?'

'They were. The dose he took would have killed an elephant.'

'And the doctor? How about the bottle he poured the stuff from? Was there any strychnine in that?'

'Not a drop. There had been some in the beaker he measured the draught into, and in his bag there was a small bottle which contained strychnine. He insisted it had been full when he had left his home to tend Larsen — but when we examined it, it was only half full.'

'You're holding him?'

'What else can we do? He must have administered the stuff.'

'I admit it looks like it — but you know as well as I do that he didn't. You know quite well there's something damned wrong about all this.'

'I know. But you won't ever persuade the law to believe in the supernatural.'

'I don't believe it's anything supernatural even now. Ghosts aren't in the habit of making telephone calls. No, it's normal enough — perhaps extraordinary, but quite human. It's just something which is too big for our narrow intellects to grasp.'

'Speak for your own intellect,' grunted Sharkey. 'Mine's ready to grasp anything. You may be interested to know that ballistics confirmed that the fingerprints on that gun were those of Arnolds, and also that the same gun fired the shots which killed Millicent.'

'But you can't hold Arnolds now.'

'I have no option. I'm holding both Arnolds and Moss. If this goes on much longer we'll be building a new wing onto the prison.'

Denby Collins twirled his whisky glass thoughtfully, looked at the plump inspector, and said: 'Sharkey, I happen to know something which might possibly have some bearing on the case. I haven't spoken before, because I didn't know if you'd take me seriously. But now I think it's an angle you may find profitable.'

'What is it? I'll try anything which could give me a fresh lead on this thing, Collins.'

'It's a certain research chemist employed by Public Promotions. The name's Calthorp. He was reported as missing from his home to your department a few days ago.'

'Missing from his home?'

'Just that. In my opinion, if you find Calthorp you'll go a long way towards shedding some light on the case.'

'Is there any special reason which makes you think that?'

'No, no special reason. Just a hunch.

And the circumstances of his disappearance were peculiar.'

Sharkey directed a sulphurous glare at him. He said, 'So! You aren't content with seeing me tripped up and tied down by five stinking murder mysteries, are you? You want me to chase after some old crank of a chemist in my spare time!'

'Only because I think it has a bearing — '

'Bearing, my left eyebrow! I've enough on my plate without chasing wild geese. If it's possible to find him, he'll be found through the usual channels, without any intervention from me. I've got my own job to worry about.'

Collins made a gesture with his hands and said, 'All right. If you want to be stubborn.'

Sharkey mopped down more whisky. He said, 'Why not leave the matter to me? If I thought the disappearance of some old fool had anything to do with the case, I'd investigate it. But I think you'll find it's just coincidence. I came here to give you the stop-press developments, and to ask your advice.'

'And I gave it to you,' pointed out Denby. 'And you're too thick-headed to take it.'

Sharkey snorted. 'It isn't a question of pig-headedness. I don't think it has a bearing, and that's all that matters.'

'If that's the way you feel, Inspector, all right. I still mean to follow that clue up myself. It seems to me you must be fond of reading about the incompetence of the police in the newspapers, otherwise you'd try every possibility.'

'All right, all right. I'll give special instructions for an effort to be made to locate this man Calthorp. But I wager when he is found it won't have any bearing on the murders.'

'And I'll wager it will, when — and *if* — he's found!'

7

The Last of the Six

Colonel Harris Gore-Blatherington opened his eyes and blinked at the early morning sunshine streaming through the curtains of his window. His eyes wandered down to the clock on the bedside table, and he uttered an exclamation of annoyance when he noted the hands pointed to nine a.m.

He came from the bed like a man on springs; he always did things that way. He stood in his heliotrope pyjamas, sniffing the morning air from the open windows, and prodding his hands against his slight pot belly. Then he commenced his setting up exercises, firmly convinced that a man should never neglect his personal health, and power of improving himself with frugal meals, and hard work. His muscular arms shot up above his head, then down to his sides; they spread out like the sails of a windmill; they jerked forwards in the attitude of a sleepwalker; they rested on his hips. He then lay down on his back, hoisted his plumpish legs in mid-air, and began to waggle each one energetically. He was supposed to be performing the motions of one riding a bike — but he resembled more strongly a semi-deformed crab in an epileptic fit!

This unusual spectacle proceeded for five minutes by the clock; he then stood up, shot both arms straight up, and swept downwards in a futile effort to touch his toes. A great gasp of wind escaped from him as his paunch got in the way and was crushed up like a fat concertina. He tried again, but in vain; it was useless. He heaved a regretful sigh, shrugged his shoulders, and walked over to the slightly open window. He flung this wide and took in great gulps of air through his nose, expelling it through his lips. He made a noise like a rhinoceros wallowing in two feet of muddy water.

Then he visited his full-length mirror and reviewed his soldierly figure as if he were inspecting the guards at Buckingham Palace. Evidently he approved of

what he saw, for a murmur of approbation left his lips, and he twirled the
ends of his white mustachios with some
abandon.

'Damn fine figure of a man, b'gad!
Fifty-five not out, by Jove. Shows what a
man can do for himself if he looks after
his health!'

It was a pity, he reflected, that his hair
on top *wasn't*. The round, bald patch up
there was a source of continual irritation
to him. He applied any and every hair
restorer he could get hold of, and had,
some years back, actually succeeded in
coaxing that bald patch to sprout a fine
layer of fuzz. But, alas, this had quickly
dropped out again, leaving him balder
than ever.

He applied brush and comb to the
scanty hair behind each ear. Then,
ejecting his head from the room door, he
bellowed, '*Hoy!* Damn and blast you,
Perkiss, why aren't you up? What kind of
a blank-blank batman d'ye call yourself? I
said eight. It's quarter past nine now.
Where's my shower, man?'

Perkiss had been his batman in India,

and on his retirement had remained with the colonel. Not that he wanted to himself — but mainly because, when the colonel suggested it, he could not find the courage to refuse. He was completely domineered by those angry red eyes under those bushy brows, and was a perfect batman for the type of master he had. No one else would have stood for the colonel's tantrums a single day.

Perkiss came out of the next room with a rush, rubbing sleep from his eyes. He mumbled, 'Blimey — sorry. I mean, good morning, sir. I didn't 'ear the bloomin' clock go orf.'

'Blast you, man,' bellowed the Colonel. 'I'll have you court-martialled — I'll have you shot at dawn! Go and run my shower! This wouldn't have done in India. I suppose you think you can take liberties here, eh, eh?'

Perkiss made himself scarce and could be heard running the shower. The colonel took a walk down the passage and turned into his wife's room. She was asleep, her rather weary-looking face deep in the pillow. The Colonel caught her a hard slap on the rump and bawled, 'Helen, how many times have I to tell you, you ought to be up and about in the morning, eh, eh? Look at me!'

'I am looking,' said his wife acidly, coming to life. 'You look perfectly revolting in those pyjamas, Harris. Must you wander about the house like that in the middle of the night?'

'Middle of the night? What? B'gad, woman, it's long past reveille now. I hopped in to ask you if you'd care to come for a gallop down the Row — eh, eh?'

'Oh, do go away, Harris. Sometimes I almost wish you were back in the Service. These last ten years have been hell with you around.'

'Strong language, m'dear,' said Colonel Gore-Blatherington with a frown. 'Very strong. Mustn't make statements like that in front of the children. Mustn't use words like 'hell', either.'

'I'm afraid I've picked that up off you, dear. If you treat me and the children as if we were army recruits, you must expect us to speak and act like them. Now *do* go away — Perkiss will ride with you.'

The colonel didn't argue. Certainly he had a great deal of his own way with his wife and son and daughter; but when she really put her foot down, she generally managed to put it right on his corn. She could be particularly nasty on occasion, and obviously this was going to be an occasion if he persisted in annoying her. He left the room. He took his shower and dressed, singing a rather blue ditty from the days when he had been the pride and joy of the officers' mess at Punjari.

If we seem to be giving undue prominence to these mundane events in the ordinary routine of one of Colonel Gore-B's mornings, we have reason — the reason being that this was the last morning he was destined to perform his time-honoured rites. For before the night fell again, Colonel Gore-Blatherington would be *dead*!

Happily unconscious of his impending doom, the colonel carolled merrily as he dressed, then moved briskly down the stairs into the breakfast room. Over a hearty meal he read his mail; then, relaxing into an armchair for a brief read before embarking upon the ride, he picked up the daily newspaper and glanced at the headlines.

At once some of the joviality faded from his face. His eyes hardened; his mustachios fairly bristled. The headline ran:

'FIFTH STRANGE DEATH IN FEW DAYS. ANOTHER OF THE DIRECTORS OF PUBLIC PROMOTIONS SAVAGELY MURDERED! POLICE COMPLETELY BAFFLED!'

He read down the two-column spread thoughtfully; then he sat gazing into space for a few minutes. At length he muttered, 'By gad! Larsen gone too! That means I'm the only remaining member of the board!' He laid down the newspaper and stood up. He rang for Perkiss, who came on the double. He said, 'My life's in danger, Perkiss.'

Perkiss stood silently by. The colonel roared, 'Well? Say something, you fool.'

'Very good, sir. Er, I mean I'm sorry to hear it.'

'I don't believe you're sorry at all, damn it,' bellowed the colonel. 'Never mind. Perkiss, go and load my old Army revolver — jildi. Bring it back to me here. By gad, if anyone attempts to kill me they'll be extremely unlucky. There's nothing worse than Fuzzy-Wuzzies, is there, Perkiss? And I've been up against them often enough, eh, eh?'

'Not 'arf, sir. I'll go and get your gun.'

He vanished from sight, and the colonel strode to the open French windows and gazed out. A somewhat weird sight met his eyes. It was in the shape of a large and round gentleman who was walking up the drive towards the front door. His face wore such an expression of woe that Colonel Gore-Blatherington wondered if he were an advance undertaker looking for business.

The colonel stepped through the window on to the terrace and yelled, '*Hoy!* Who're you? What do you want here?'

Chief Inspector Sharkey wheeled slowly; turning round was rather a big manoeuvre to one of Sharkey's bulk, and in the process several border flowers were mercilessly trampled on. But he nodded to the colonel and walked towards him, stomach wobbling with every step.

'Good morning, sir,' he began. 'I am

Chief Inspector Sharkey from Scotland Yard.'

'A policeman,' grunted the Colonel. 'Damn, I might have known it. Those feet — that Derby — that expression. Typical!'

Sharkey winced but carried on bravely, 'I have called on you to inform you that we intend to give you police protection.'

'What?' barked the colonel grimly.

'Police protection, Colonel. I have detailed two men to look after you.'

For a moment the colonel could only stare. Then a bull-like roar escaped him. 'You're what? Why, damn you, sir, I like your confounded impudence! I'm a grown man, fully capable of protecting myself! If anyone needs protection I think it's your damned tribe of Yard men!'

Sharkey said valiantly, 'I suppose you know you're in danger?'

'I can guess it. But may I add I've been in danger before? From Fuzzy-Wuzzies, sir, and they're *damned* dangerous. I have no doubts of my ability to protect myself. I was the finest marksman in the Lancers!'

'It isn't a question of Fuzzy-Wuzzies,' said Sharkey, almost with a sneer. 'It's a question of something . . . uncanny.'

'There couldn't be anything more uncanny than those damned Fuzzy-Wuzzies, sir. They spring up from nowhere, and before you can say Calcutta, you're surrounded.'

'But this is an unseen menace. You've read the newspapers, haven't you, Colonel? You know how your fellow directors have met their ends?'

'I do, sir. But I believe the people concerned must have been either blind or simple. I guarantee you that if anyone tries anything with me, they'll be sorry. Mark my words.'

'I see. I take it then that you refuse police protection?'

'I certainly do. If I see any policeman within a mile of me I'll have them court-martialled, sir. Snooping into people's affairs!'

'As you wish. While I am here I'd like to ask you one or two questions which may have some bearing on the case. Mr. Larsen told me that probably you would be able to recall the names of some of the people who have a perpetual grudge against you and your friends. Some unscrupulous person who might wish to murder you six?'

The colonel reflected, and said finally, 'At the moment I can think of only one man who may have considered he had a motive for killing us. I cannot tell you the reason — but I can tell you the fellow's name.'

'And that is . . . ?'

'Dr. Calthorp, sir. He is employed by us as a research chemist, but recently I understand he has failed to report for duty. In fact, ever since the first of these murders took place. That is the only man I can think of who might have a logical motive for killing the six of us — but I assure you that should he try any little games on me he will be severely dealt with.'

Sharkey looked taken aback at the words. Now he said: 'Were you aware that Dr. Calthorp has vanished?'

'Vanished?'

'Entirely. From his home. That is doubtless why he has not been in to his work.'

'Hmm. Perhaps it serves his purpose to be missing while these killings take place. Now you have told me this, I am more than ever willing to believe Calthorp is mixed up with the whole devilish business.'

'I myself wondered if he had stumbled onto anything of great importance in his work, and had mentioned it to you gentlemen. That would account for you all being murdered . . . '

'Pray don't include me yet,' snarled the colonel.

'Sorry. That would account for the other five being murdered, and the doctor vanishing. Did he tell you anything which someone else might have been anxious to know?'

'Nothing at all. Nor, to the best of my knowledge, did he tell my co-directors anything.'

'Very well. I will bear what you have said in mind, Colonel. If you are determined to refuse our protection, I would advise you to be armed and prepared at any moment — not that I consider that will help you much, but you will at least be able to put up a fight. Good day!'

Sharkey navigated a flowerbed without crushing more than five or six plants, and crunched back down the drive again.

Outside he signalled to a closed car, which drove up. He said, 'He may be attacked at any moment now. Keep your eyes on this house, and if he leaves follow on. Don't lose touch with him. If anything does happen call me immediately. I'll be at the Yard.'

The two men in the car nodded, and Sharkey rolled off down the road. He had done his best for the colonel. If he still got killed it would hardly be Sharkey's fault.

* * *

Colonel Gore-Blatherington reined in his horse and regarded the lie of the land before him. He had ventured farther afield than had been his intention, travelling merely at walking pace and enjoying the clean, fresh tang of the morning. His horse was getting old, having been with him for many years during his army days, and was no longer fit for galloping. Even the slow pace had told on Ali, and his tongue hung out as the colonel dismounted on the heath and tethered him to an out-jutting tree branch.

The colonel leaned against the trunk, and took from his pocket his pipe and matches. Idly he filled it, thinking of nothing in particular. He was comfortingly assured of the squat hardness of his loaded army pistol in his pocket, and he meant to use it, when and if it should be necessary.

He had almost smoked a pipe through, when the horse pricked up its ears and whinnied. Suddenly it reared in fear, and the colonel gazed at it with mild surprise. Ali seldom showed any fear of anything. A mount which was used to having a horde of yelling, black-faced, fuzzy-haired demons jumping out waving krisses in the Indian night had to be really badly frightened to show any reaction. But Ali was showing a definite reaction!

The horse was now pulling at its reins and glaring at a spot just before the colonel with distended eyes. The colonel followed its gaze, but failed to see anything other than the green, rolling heath and the tall grass.

Then he stiffened; his eyes became fixed to a section of grass not two yards away, which rustled for no reason — *there was no wind*.

He noticed that just above the moving grasses the view was not so clear — it was warped, blurred, as if viewed through a sheet of distorting glass. He tensed, and his hand clutched the gun in his pocket.

The grasses stirred again, then became suddenly motionless.

The colonel stared for minutes, failing to hear a stealthy rustle in the leaves of the tree above him. The first warning of approaching danger came in the form of a taut noose of rope, which snaked down and settled round his neck. Automatically his gun hand snapped from his pocket, but before he could gauge his line of fire, he was hauled, choking, into the air. The revolver exploded twice, aimlessly . . .

★　★　★

Denby Collins said, 'What was that?'

He drew in his mount, and Sheila Calthorp drew in hers beside him. The two were spending a pleasant morning on the heath, riding, with Denby trying to take her attention off her father's strange disappearance. He had phoned for the date and Sheila had been only too willing. In the course of an hour they had found out quite a lot about each other.

And then the shots had shattered into their consciousness, and had made them both suddenly jump, with a premonition of evil somewhere ahead.

The girl said, 'Perhaps it's someone hunting rabbits?'

He shook his head and said, 'Those were revolver shots, or I'm getting hard of hearing. Come on, let's see.'

They spurred their horses on, over the ridge ahead and down into a valley by a clump of trees. Long before they reached the spot they knew what that hanging body portended; and they were too late to help the colonel. He was quite dead when they arrived. Denby cut him down and said, 'Who the devil . . . ?'

Two men had approached unseen from the rear. One said, 'It's Colonel Gore-Blatherington. We're detectives from Headquarters. You're Collins, aren't you, sir? We've seen you with Chief Inspector

Sharkey. We were supposed to follow this man, but when he came on to the heath we had to leave the car and follow on foot. Is he dead?'

'He's dead,' said Denby, nodding. '*The last of the six!*'

8

Who's Next?

Chief Inspector Sharkey said vitriolically, 'You pair of blockheads! Didn't I tell you to follow him closely? Didn't I? Then how did he get so far ahead?'

The two plain clothes men looked uncomfortable, and one of them said, 'It wasn't our fault, sir. We had to leave the car at the beginning of the heath and follow on foot. If there was anyone after him we didn't want to be conspicuous, so we kept a fair way in the rear. About a hundred yards or so. He wasn't going fast, and we lost sight of him for a minute. We saw him leaning against this tree trunk, smoking. We kept under cover and watched, and without any warning of any description he suddenly rose in the air . . . We hurried to him as fast as we could, but it was too late. Mr. Collins and the young lady were here before us, and even they weren't in time.'

Sharkey sighed and said, 'Did *you* see anyone about, Collins?'

'Not a soul, Inspector. We were over the ridge when we heard him fire two shots. We galloped down here and found him strung up on the tree. There wasn't anyone with him at all. Then your men came hurrying up.'

'I suppose it's the same man behind this who's been behind the other crimes. Ah, well, at least the colonel's the last of the six. Perhaps now we can hope for a bit of peace . . . '

Denby Collins doubted it, but said nothing.

It was some time before they left the scene of the murder, and then they didn't feel like riding any longer. Denby suggested they should go home and change, meeting later at the Savoy Grille for lunch, and to this Sheila agreed.

They met at the appointed time, and after picking listlessly at her food, Sheila said, 'Denby, have you found out anything about Father? Those notes you took?'

He shook his head and said, 'No. I haven't heard from my friend Sylvester yet. I'm expecting him to call any time now though, and then we may get a long way towards solving the mystery surrounding your father. By the way, Sharkey had a word in private with me while we were down there this morning. He said Colonel Gore-Blatherington had informed him that your father would have had reason for wishing to murder the directors of Public Promotions. He wouldn't say why, and I wondered if you knew anything about it?'

Her eyes had an amazed look. She said, 'Good heavens, Denby, they surely don't suspect Father?'

Denby shrugged and said, 'You know Sharkey — he suspects everybody. But it might help if we knew what the colonel was driving at when he made the insinuation.'

She frowned and said, 'I think I can tell you that — but you must treat it confidentially. Honestly, Denby, I swear to you I know Father better than to think for one minute he'd go round killing those men just because of something which happened years ago. At the time he was working for the same firm, and he had an agreement that for anything he produced as research chemist for them, which was saleable and brought in over a certain amount of profit, they would pay to him a sum of ten percent over and above his wage.

'He did invent something which proved invaluable, and from which the firm made hundreds of thousands — but they didn't honour their contract to give him ten percent, and he couldn't enforce his claim as he only had their word for it. He discovered a cure for common cold, which sells all over the world, and which is known by the name of Shiftit. I think it is the firm's only real claim to fame, and Father never touched a penny more than his wages.'

'Did he take them to court?'

'No. They threatened him with dismissal, and at the time he had me to support, and he daren't offend them. So he simply went on working for them, but he vowed the next time he got onto anything worthwhile he'd use it for his own profit. That would be what the colonel meant when he said Father had a grudge against them all. For they were all in the plot to cheat him of his commission.'

'I think I understand. You're sure your father wouldn't be the kind to take revenge on them — not even if he found a safe way?'

'Not even then. I know he wouldn't, Denby. He's far too gentle.'

But Denby wondered. He knew quite well how emotionally unstable a genius could be; knew that excessive effort and incessant study could unhinge a man's mental balance, and convert him from mouse into monster. He wondered if anything of that nature had occurred in the case of Calthorp — but he wisely said nothing of his suspicions to Sheila.

The entire board of directors of Public Promotions had met with ghastly deaths within a short space of time of the doctor's mysterious disappearance. Terror had struck, and the Yard was baffled. They had died weirdly and horribly, and the farther into the case Denby went, the more he was sure their deaths were not due to anything supernatural.

He said, 'Is there anyone else who might possibly know what your father was working on?'

She considered for a moment; then she said, 'Why, yes, he had a woman working with him as assistant down at the firm's lab. A Miss Angela Taylor. I didn't ever meet her, but he often mentioned her to me. He disapproved of her strongly as far as I could gather. She was the flirty type, making eyes at all the other chemists, and paying little or no attention to her job. But as I said, Father was far too kind-hearted to complain about her.'

'Do you happen to know her address?'

She shook her head. 'I think you'd have to find out that from the general manager down at the firm's factory.'

Denby nodded, took a note of the name, and then talked of other things to take the matter off her mind. It was almost four o'clock before they rose to leave, when he called a taxi outside and said, 'I hope you won't mind me leaving you like this, but I want to get in touch with this girl Taylor before the place shuts down for the day. I'll ring you tonight about eight. All right?'

He watched her cab roll away, then called himself a second cab and directed it to proceed to the Public Promotions manufacturing plant. This was situated in a dirty-looking district in the Wapping area. It was a tall, gloomy building with little of the modern about it. It had originally been a derelict warehouse until Señor Ventura, seeking a cheap location for his factory, had taken it over, done some minor repairs, and converted it into a general factory for the manufacture of various commodities.

Work was in full swing when Denby pushed open the green door which led to the timekeeper's office and said, 'I'd like to speak to the manager if I may.'

The walrus-moustached man said, 'You can leave a message, chum. Manager's busy supervising the new foot ointment.'

Denby slipped a five-pound note over to him, and the walrus-moustached gent clawed it into his keeping and said, 'I can't leave me post — the workmen have a habit of slipping out for fags when I do that — but if you walk in here, take the first right, and the second left, you'll come into the vats. That's the room where they boil this ointment they're making. You'll find him there. It's a new process they're trying, and he'll be supervising the first batch. If he asks, tell him you sneaked past me, will you, mister?'

Denby nodded and pushed open the inner swing door; he entered into the depressing atmosphere of the despatch room, and several workmen looked at him curiously, then returned to their jobs. As if he was the chairman paying a flying visit, Denby strolled on unconcernedly.

The room the doorkeeper had called the vats was a high, long, cavern-like affair. Along both sides ran vast containers like the vats in breweries, but slightly smaller. On these vats men were standing and looking down into a haze of steam and fumes which rose from the boiling liquid.

Standing on the nearest vat to him, balanced delicately on a foot-wide rim round the top, examining a watch, stood a man in a lounge suit, and with an air of authority. Denby assumed him to be the manager, and walked over in that direction. He called, 'Hello up there!'

The manager looked down at him through a curtain of smoke and said, 'Well?'

Denby called, 'I'm from Scotland Yard — I'd like to ask you one or two questions if I may.'

'Sure,' called the other. 'I'll be down in a minute or two. Got to keep an eye on this first . . . No, don't come up. You aren't used to it — might lose your footing, and it wouldn't be pleasant to fall into a vat full of boiling mud, which is what this stuff resembles at the moment.'

Denby waited patiently until the other snapped shut his watch and pulled a lever by his side. Then he turned and began to walk carefully round the rim, with the sure step of one who has done the tricky balancing act many times and is in no danger of slipping.

And suddenly, for no apparent reason, he gave a wild shriek and threw his hands up, clawing at thin air. Then, with a last despairing cry, he plunged headforemost into the boiling, glutinous substance in the vat!

Denby was up the iron ladder in seconds and stepped onto the rim, gazing down in horror at the yellow, smelly, bubbling mess below . . .

No one could have fallen into that steaming ointment and still survived. Of the manager there was no sign — only the glucking of the viscous liquid below.

Others had seen, and now the first arrival ran up the ladder. 'Christ!' he exclaimed. 'The poor b . . . ' He peered into the boiling mess and shouted down to his mates, 'Get Joe to stop the boilers — tell Eddie to drain this lot off through the rear pipe.' A scene of frenzied activity started below, and the workman said: ''*ell!* Fancy 'im slipping down after orl the times 'e's been up 'ere.'

'He didn't slip, in my opinion,' said Denby slowly. 'I think he was pushed!'

'Pushed? You're crazy, mate. I saw 'im slip meself. There wasn't nobody up 'ere to push 'im, was there?' The man gazed down, bending precariously over the vat. He said, 'Not a ruddy 'ide nor 'air of 'im. 'e's a gonner all right. Fair put the wind up me when I sees anyone go into a vat like this . . . 'ell! Oo're you pushing, mate?'

He straightened up and glared at Denby. Denby said, 'I didn't push — I felt someone push past me, though.'

The man gazed blankly along the rim towards the ladder. He saw no one; but Denby, following his gaze, seemed to see a warp in the view — a distorted effect just above the ladder, such as takes place when steam rises from a kettle of boiling water, or heat rises from the surface of a stove. It was gone as suddenly as it had come, and it left him wondering if it had been some trick of the fumes from the vat.

The workman was now regarding him curiously. He said, 'You don't work 'ere, mate, do you?'

'No. I came along to see — well, to see the man who just fell into that vat. He was the general manager, wasn't he?'

'Yes; 'e was a bad swine, too, although I don't oughter speak no evil of the dead. But 'e was an 'oly terror, take my tip. Was 'e a friend of yours?'

'No, no. I just wanted to ask him about something.'

'Oh. Well you can't ask 'im now, can you?'

Denby shook his head. He said, 'You may think his fall was due to a slip — but I'm sure it was *murder*. I'd advise you to get in touch with Chief Inspector Sharkey of Scotland Yard!' Then he walked carefully — very carefully — away towards the ladder. He had no desire to wait until the vat had been drained, and exposed its gruesome contents.

He left the room without attracting much attention and found his way back to the front office. He said to the door-keeper, 'I'd like to know where I can find the research department.'

'Research? First on the left down here.'

He thanked the doorman, walked down the passage again, and turned as directed. There was no mistake about it; he was right for the research. Gilt letters on a frosted glass door said: 'LABORATORY — Keep Out'.

Denby went in.

There were the usual benches, test tubes, retorts, colour screens, sinks, and the customary scientific paraphernalia used in work of the kind Public Promotions was engaged in. Three or four chemists looked up as he entered, and one came over and said, 'Looking for someone?'

Denby lied calmly. 'I'm from the Yard — Scotland Yard. I want to see a young lady called, er, Angela Taylor. She here?'

'Angela? Good God, what's the kid done?'

'She's done nothing. I simply want to ask her a question or two.'

'Yes, she's here. You'll find her over in the corner at Calthorp's bench. He isn't here, and she's working on one or two notes he left for her. Watch your step — she's a bit of a wench!'

Denby nodded and crossed over behind the benches to the corner. A red-haired, green-eyed girl, with voluptuous curves which even her plain overall didn't conceal, was dipping test samples of cloth into a bowl of dye. Denby said, 'Miss Taylor? Sorry to butt in like this, but it's about Dr. Calthorp.'

She said, eagerly looking up, 'Where is he? Have you found him?'

'Not yet — but I hoped you'd be able

to assist me by answering a few questions.'

Her green eyes narrowed. She said, 'Are you a policeman?'

'No, just a friend of his. But does it matter?'

'I don't think I know you, do I?'

'I'm sure you don't. My name's Collins — Denby Collins.'

'Not — not the famous author?' she gasped, eyes wide.

'I wouldn't say famous — but I am an author. Turned detective just at the moment. Will you help?'

She hesitated, then seemed to decide abruptly. She said, 'I'd love to help. Dr. Calthorp was kind to me. I'm rather lazy, I admit that, and he probably had good reason for having me fired more than once. But he didn't report me. I can't answer questions here, now. But if I can see you tonight . . . ?'

'That would be fine. Will you come to my place, or shall we go out somewhere?'

'I think if you'd come along to my place, it would be better. I have an apartment in Brixton. Holland Road.

Here's the address.' She rummaged in her pocket, produced paper and pencil and scribbled down details. She said, 'What time can I expect you?'

'About eight? Is that all right?'

'That's perfect. Don't forget, Mr. Collins.' She smirked, and he left with the feeling that the whole thing had been her idea and not his! But whichever it was, the evening promised to be fraught with interest in more ways than one.

9

A Startling Discovery

Denby looked for the bell push with Angela Taylor on it, found it, and rang a peal. It said beneath the name, 'Flat Three', and since this was the top flat, Denby didn't expect to be let in at once. He wasn't.

In fact, there was quite a wait — so long a wait that he rather impatiently thumbed the bell again. Then he heard steps descending the stairs, and the door opened; Angela Taylor looked out. She was clad in a figure-fitting, unadorned green dress, with a single pearl necklace round her smooth white throat. She looked radiant, and smiled at him.

He said, 'You took your time. I was beginning to think you'd stood me up and gone somewhere.'

'No, I wouldn't have done anything like that. It's just that . . . Well, the truth is, a

124

friend of mine paid me an unexpected visit.'

'Pity. I hoped we'd be alone.'

She nodded. 'So did I. He wasn't supposed to come — we hadn't made any arrangements for tonight. But I suppose, looking at it one way, he has the right to call any time he feels like it.'

'He has? That sounds rather strange. Relative?'

'Fiancé. But do come in, Mr. Denby. I mustn't keep you standing out here. I expect he'll go shortly.'

Denby nodded and stepped inside. He followed her up the stairs, feeling a bit uncomfortable, for it was going to be rather awkward explaining to a girl's fiancé just how it came about he was paying her a visit at night and was, presumably, intending to be alone with her in her flat.

He needn't have worried: the girl had her fiancé well under control, and although Denby detected a glint of malice in the man's eyes as he was introduced, it had gone as rapidly as a pleasant smile could make it.

The girl said, 'Mr. Denby Collins — you've heard of him, Jack? Mr. Collins, my fiancé, Jack Street.'

Denby shook hands with him politely. Street's grip was moist and flabby, the kind of handshake Denby detested. The man himself didn't seem up to much: he was thin and weedy, with sandy-coloured hair high back on his forehead. His shoulders were slightly stooped, and he sported a straggly sandy moustache, nicotine-stained. His fingers were stained with various colours, seemingly dyed into the skin. The cigarette he held twitched spasmodically. His chin receded so much that it was difficult to determine the line where throat left off and chin began. Of all his features only his nose was worthy of mention, and even that looked incongruous in the setting of his feeble face. His eyes were in character, being small and furtive.

'How are you?' said Street conventionally.

The girl said, 'Mr. Collins is looking for Dr. Calthorp. Perhaps you could help him, Jack?' She turned to Collins and

126

said, 'Jack used to work at the lab about a year ago, before he threw the job up. He worked with Dr. Calthorp — that's where I first met him.'

'Oh, I see. Perhaps you *could* help, Mr. Street.'

'If I can,' the thin man told him. 'What exactly did you want to know?'

'I wondered if you knew what lines the doctor was following? Did he mention anything in particular to you?'

Street reflected, then said, 'Far as I know he was only working on dyes — he didn't seem to be following any particular line. Just looking for new colours. Course, that was a year ago, and he may have developed something unusual since then, if that's what you mean.'

'That is what I mean. I have a firm conviction he's developed something *very* unusual, Mr. Street.'

'Then if he has it's a sure thing he'll keep it to himself. He wouldn't tell anyone else about it. You see, he had a grudge against the directors of the company — he once told me he'd kill them if he ever got the chance. They robbed him of the credit and money which his discovery would have brought him. He invented Shiftit, the common cold cure. Perhaps you've heard of it?'

'I've done more — I've used it. It does everything the proprietors claim. Shifted a bad dose of flu I picked up last year.'

'Then you'll fully realise how much Dr. Calthorp thought he was going to make on the discovery. The trick they played on him was despicable. But jobs were scarce for us chemists in the research line, and at that time he daren't resign. Pity, too, for the man was undeniably a genius. If he'd had his own well-equipped laboratory, he'd have made a fortune in no time.' Street picked up his hat from a nearby chair and said, 'Well, Angela, if you aren't coming along to the play . . . ?'

'Not tonight, Jack, dear. You run along yourself. It would be a pity to waste your money.'

'Hmm. Perhaps, as I have two seats, Mr. Denby would care to — '

'No, thanks. I don't feel very much in the play-going mood. Nice of you to offer, though. I think I'll just have a word or two with Miss Taylor, if you have no objections?'

'But of course not,' said the young man, but Denby saw the way he bit his lip, and knew he had objections although he dared not mention them in front of the girl. He said, 'Well, good night. I'll have to dash.' He looked at the girl, hesitated, then said, 'I don't suppose it'd be any use my coming back after the show, darling, would it?'

'Oh, no, Jack. Not tonight. I'm rather tired.'

'Yes, you do look worn out,' he said meaningfully. 'I'd get to bed *early* if I were you.'

The girl's lips tightened, but she said nothing. She walked out and downstairs to the door with him, and when she came back Denby had found himself a seat and was reading through a copy of one of his books which had been on the table.

She smiled at him and said, 'Oh! I see you've noticed that copy of your book. I've read it time after time — I think it's wonderful.'

He smiled back and said, 'That's rather

extraordinary. It was only published this morning!'

She flushed scarlet, laughed, then said, 'You've caught me out then, Mr. Collins. Yes, I admit it, I picked it up on the stall coming home. I didn't know it was a new title. Can you forgive me for trying to deceive you?'

'You're already forgiven — there's nothing to forgive. I'm feeling a little guilty about your young man, though.'

'Jack? Oh, he's a weak fool. I haven't any intention of marrying him. I got engaged to him for a joke more or less; and anyway, he was making good money at the time. Now he's out of work, and hasn't a cent. What's more, he doesn't seem to want work. He can't be trying, I think.'

'Then why not tell him your intentions?'

'To tell you the truth, I don't like to hurt his feelings. He's such a sensitive sort of boy, and he'd be sure to make a scene. I can't stand scenes, can you? Especially scenes which contain a lot of self-pity, and Jack would be ever so sorry for himself. I expect he'd go right to the river and make a hole in the surface.'

'But you'll have to tell him sooner or later.'

'Later. I hope to just break things off slowly, so that he thinks we've naturally drifted apart. You see, I've met someone else recently down at the lab. An awfully nice young man called Lester Burnham. We plan to get married, and he wanted to tell Jack the whole story, but I asked him not to — not yet. I just keep turning Jack down when he comes or phones for dates. He'll get tired eventually.'

Denby regarded her carefully and said, 'And what would your new prospective husband say if he was aware I was up here with you?'

'But he isn't, is he? I mean he couldn't be. And there's nothing wrong, is there? Besides, a girl must have her admirers, mustn't she?'

'You include me as one of your admirers?'

She came nearer and sat on the arm of his chair; she looked down at him from veiled eyes and murmured, '*Aren't you?*'

He said, 'I take quite a time to become fond of anyone.'

'I have a lot of spare time on my hands. Do you think you could learn?'

'I think you're forgetting exactly why I came,' he told her, suddenly ginning. 'I came to *ask* questions — not answer them. I think if we confine ourselves to that, we shouldn't be in any danger of getting fond of one another.'

'Oh, Mr. Collins.' She pouted. 'Or may I call you Denby?'

'You can call me Father Christmas if you like,' he told her. 'As long you don't get active.'

She offered him a cigarette from a green shagreen case, and lit one for herself. She gave that to him, red with her lipstick, and took his. She smoked it, and he smoked hers. She said, 'You know, I think men are adorable. I love them, the quaint creatures. Every man is different, and I do adore getting on really intimate terms with them, and seeing just how each one reacts.'

'How have I reacted?' he asked quizzically, eyebrow raised.

'Unsatisfactorily. Up to the moment.'

'And that's the way it's going to stay. I thought you wished to help locate Calthorp?'

'I do. But since you're so hard, I must set a price on my information.'

'A price?'

'Yes. I'd love to know what it's like to be kissed by a real live author.'

'No different from being kissed by a chimney sweep,' he told her. 'Perhaps not as passionate.'

She crossed her legs and blew smoke at him lazily. She said, 'Well, that's my price for information. I must break down your coldness before you go, Denby darling. What do you say?'

He said, 'If that's what you want you can have it. I expect you think one kiss will lead to another, and once a man's touched your lips he wouldn't be able to draw back. I'll have to prove you wrong, Angela. Anyway, if the information's worth the kiss, I'll give it you *after* you've talked. All right?'

She nodded and said, 'I'll take your word. I expect you think I'm an outrageous flirt?'

'You *are* an outrageous flirt,' he asserted. 'But I don't hold it against you. It's one way of getting fun out of life. I might even have enjoyed playing along if I didn't happen to have my eye on a certain young lady already.'

'I won't ask who she is — I don't suppose you'd tell me anyway. The kiss'll satisfy me . . . ' She said suddenly, 'You — you don't think I'm awfully cheap, do you, Denby?'

'No.' He smiled. 'You're far too naïve to be bad at heart. I know you just like being different, having innocent fun. Am I right?'

'Of course you are. I like talking to you — you understand. I've tried to analyse myself, and I've come to the conclusion that I like to *think* I'm bad. It's really rather childish, isn't it?'

'Aren't people always childish when they're having fun?'

She lit another cigarette and said, 'I love you for saying that, Denby. You *do* understand me. And I really did feel very fond of old Dr. Calthorp — he was so kind to me, although he knew what a lazy person I was. I can't tell you a lot, but what I do know is that he had discovered some new kind of dye which he claimed would make the whole scientific world sit up and start revising their theories. He dashed home early to complete his tests, for it was common knowledge he didn't intend to hand any of his formulae over to the firm again. That's the last I saw of him.'

'And you are unaware what the nature of the dye was?'

'I only know it was very, very unusual.' She went to the cupboard, brought out a bottle of cheap wine and said, 'It isn't the kind you'd get at the Ritz, but it isn't bad once you've tasted it. Puts a cast-iron lining on your throat. Will you have a drink, Denby?'

He nodded absently; he was thinking hard. To him the whole case was shaping up exactly the way he had figured it out earlier. She came back with two glasses, and stood them at his elbow. Then she bent over the chair, took his face in her hands, and pressed her lips to his.

Denby put an arm about her shoulders.

He wasn't looking for an affair with her, but he could hardly sit stonily while she kissed him. On top of that he knew quite well there was no harm behind her thoughts, as there was none behind his. It was an adventure; a minor chance to escape from reality for a minute, to live in a world of false glamour and unexpectedness. A game to enliven her dull life of routine.

His eyes gazed past her cheek to the door, which had opened softly. He suddenly pushed her away, startled.

'Oh, Denny, don't be so cold . . . ' She pouted; then she saw his fixed look and stared behind her at the door. 'Oh!' she said, subdued. '*Lester*, er, what made you call?'

The young man in the doorway was one of the square-jawed, stern-featured kind, who was obviously rocked to his boots by the knowledge that his sweetheart could possibly deign to kiss anyone lesser than himself. Denby recognised him for one of the men he had seen working in the lab of Public Promotions that afternoon. He strode into the room, and in a bitter voice said, 'Angela! How — how *could* you? This — this is the *end!*'

She coloured, then came back: 'Oh, for God's sake, don't be so damnably dramatic, Lester. I was only kissing him . . .'

'I know,' said Lester tragically. 'But would it have stopped at a kiss?'

She flared up immediately, and Denby groaned, for the remark had brought out all her temper and lessened chances of smoothing things over. She snapped, 'Why you — you insufferable prig, Lester. How *dare* you infer that is — is — well, what you *did* infer?'

'What else am I to infer?' rapped the young man, scowling at the floor as if he expected the carpet to jump and bite him. 'When I pay you an unexpected visit, and find — *this!*'

Denby stood up and said, 'If you're referring to me as 'this', you'd better let me introduce myself. My name is Denby Collins.'

'A friend of mine,' put in the girl. 'An old friend. He writes books on ghosts and things.'

'Really? And what are you? One of the

things?' He ducked with a pained expression as the green cigarette-case whizzed past his ear and collided against the door jamb. He said stiffly, 'I can see when I'm not wanted. I'll leave.'

Denby said, 'Now just a minute. There isn't any need for anyone to leave except me. Perhaps I can explain — Angela is my cousin.'

'Cousin?' stammered the young man.

'I said cousin,' lied Denby amiably. 'I haven't seen her for some time, and she was merely giving me a cousinly kiss. It's the custom in our family.'

'I — I didn't know she had a — a cousin?'

'Well, you know now,' snapped Angela, playing up. 'And I should think you're terribly ashamed of yourself, making such a scene!'

'I — I am. I'm — I'm sorry, Collins. I had no idea — look here, forgive me, will you?'

'That's for Angela to say,' replied Denby, picking up his hat. 'I should think you'd have to do quite a lot of apologising before she's willing to overlook what you said. I'm off now. Good night.'

Angela said: 'I'll see you to the door, Denny. You wait here for me, you worm,' she snapped at Lester, and he subsided into the chair Denby had just quitted.

They walked down the stairs together, and Denby said, 'If I were you, and you're really fond of that young man, I'd play the game with him entirely.'

'I will, Denby. I really do love him. I'll telephone Jack tonight — he'll be hurt, but best to make a clean break. And — and thank you ever so much for — for explaining for me.'

And before he could stop her she had kissed him again. He grinned, shook his head, and wagged a finger at her. 'I think that young man is going to lead a very worried life with you,' he told her. Then with a wave he started back for his apartments.

He found the elegant Miss Volt correcting the proofs of his latest in his study. As he came in, she glanced up and said, 'So there you are. What have you been doing — fighting?'

'Not at all.' He smiled. 'Why?'

'Then if you haven't been fighting, I'd advise you to wipe that lipstick off your face. It makes you look as though you've been hunting for trouble in Limehouse.' She sniffed and continued her corrections as he rubbed at the offending smears with his handkerchief. But she hadn't finished with him yet. She said, 'Whoever's been kissing you must use red paint on her lips. Who was it?'

'Jealous?' He grinned.

'Who, me? Good heavens, no! Only I use a rather tasty brand of lipstick myself. If you must go native, why leave home to do it?'

He said, 'Miss Volt, kindly remember your position. You work for me; you're under my protection. And in any case you know you haven't anything more than a maternal sort of affection for me.'

She sighed and said, 'You're right at that. I spend most of my time getting you out of jams with other women.'

'You do — you're an angel. But it won't last much longer. I'm going to get married — if she'll have me.'

Miss Volt said distastefully, 'Ugh! I

suppose you imagine she'll allow you to retain your present staff of good-looking maids and a passable secretary?'

'I'm sure she will — she's an understanding sort of girl. But we'll see.'

Miss Volt said, 'Who's the unlucky woman?'

'You don't know her — a Miss *Sheila Calhorp*!'

10

The Secret Out

At ten-thirty that same evening, a young man staggered down the stairs from Angela Taylor's flat. One side of his head was bathed in blood, which dripped down on to his collar; his wild, staring eyes searched dementedly for the telephone, and found it on a small stand in the hall. He grasped the receiver and gave the number of Scotland Yard.

Scotland Yard took his incoherent call, and contrived to make sense of his fumbling explanations. Following instructions, a call was at once put through to Chief Inspector Sharkey, who ordered them to send men down and not to move anything until he arrived. He in turn put through a call to Denby Collins, and Miss Volt put it through to the writer on the extension which led to the library, where he was reading.

Ten minutes later Sharkey's car called for him, and the two were whisked away to the address Denby had so recently left.

Denby said, 'But what's happened?'

'Better wait until we get there — I don't know a great deal myself yet. We won't be long now.'

They weren't long; they drew up before the house, and Denby gasped, 'Good God, Inspector — nothing's happened to Miss Taylor, has it?'

'Yes, it has. You know her?'

'Why, yes. I only left the apartment a short time ago. What — what's happened?'

'What generally happens in London these days? She's been murdered, that's what.'

Denby, looking slightly dazed, led the way upstairs to the door of the girl's flat. It was open, and a covey of Yard men were taking photographs, fingerprints, and examining a poker which was soaked with fresh blood. An agitated landlady stood weeping in one corner; and on a chair, with a blank, unbelieving stare on his features, sat Lester Burnham. He was holding a blood-soaked handkerchief to his face and was being watched by a stout constable.

Sharkey said, 'Where's the body?'

'Behind the settee where it fell, Inspector. You said it hadn't to be disturbed.'

Sharkey and Denby went round, and stood gazing in horror at the blood-smeared mess which had once been a young and pretty woman. Sharkey said, 'What's the verdict, Hallam?'

The police doctor said, 'I should think it's obvious how she died — been dead about twenty minutes. Head and face battered with blunt instrument, presumably the poker.'

Sharkey grunted and looked at the poker, which had been laid in a handkerchief on the table. Then he turned to the wretched man in the chair and said, 'You the fellow who put the call in?' Burnham nodded. Sharkey said, 'How'd you come to kill her?'

Burnham shook his head, almost automatically. He said, 'I didn't kill her. It happened this way. Mr. Denby had been gone a long time, and we'd been having a quarrel. Then she told me she wouldn't ever have any men up to her room again, and said she'd phone Street later and tell him everything was off between them. We made it up then, and she went to sleep on my arm. It was about ten minutes later when I felt something strike me on the head. That's all I knew until I came round and found her lying there, with the poker beside her.'

'Who's this Street you mentioned?'

'Jack Street. He was her fiancé, but she didn't mean to marry him. She said she was going to phone him later.' His voice was toneless and mechanical, like a monotonous phonograph record.

'So you'd been quarrelling?'

'Yes.'

'It wouldn't be possible that in the excitement you lost your head and beat her like this, would it? That smack you got yourself might have been caused by the girl trying to defend herself.'

'I didn't. I've told you the truth.'

'Could anyone have sneaked in here without you seeing them?'

'They must have done.'

'But if you were sitting on the settee, facing the door, how could they have done?'

He shook his head helplessly. He said: 'I've told you all I can. My head's splitting. Please leave me alone.'

Denby drew the inspector aside and said, 'I believe him, Sharkey. The kid's racked up with that smack he's had. He's struggling to keep control of himself.'

'I half-believe him myself — but he had motive and opportunity. And circumstantial evidence compels me to hold him.'

'You're certainly going to need that new wing to the gaol,' Denby told him.

Sharkey grunted. 'You think this is another of the same killings?'

'What else? The girl worked down at the laboratory of Public Promotions, didn't she? And didn't the manager get his this very afternoon?'

Sharkey scowled. 'So he did. But that's *supposed* to be an accident. For God's sake, don't make things any worse than they are. He has to go in — but we'll handle him with kid gloves, don't worry.'

Denby strolled over to the bemused

chemist and said, 'Don't take it too hard. They're going to arrest you, but I think I can promise you won't be in long. I've got an angle . . .'

'I don't care what they do with me,' he said tonelessly. 'Now she's . . . dead.'

A plain clothes man came over, holding handcuffs. Denby said, 'You won't need those.'

Sharkey called, 'That's right. Don't cuff him; he's in no condition to resist.'

The plain clothes man jerked Burnham to his feet and yanked him towards the door. They went out. Sharkey prowled round the room examining everything he could spot.

The fingerprint man said, 'No prints on the poker, sir.'

'None? Hmm. I suppose he could have wiped them off. All right, Ailson, check the doorknob and the wine glasses.'

'What are you going to all this trouble for?' demanded Denby. 'You know as well as I do he didn't do it.'

Sharkey threw him a glare and snarled, 'I asked you down here, but don't get in my hair.'

'*Which* hair?' said Denby innocently.

'The law has to take its course,' Sharkey snapped. 'And it's going to.'

'Oh, yes,' agreed Denby. 'There have been seven unexplained murders in London, but the law still has to take its course, and steadfastly turns a deaf ear to any suggestions which might put them on the right track.'

'I'm not turning any deaf ears,' Sharkey told him. 'If you've anything to say, say it.'

'I will. *Find Dr. Calthorp!*'

'Pah!' snorted Sharkey. 'I haven't time to go rounding up absent-minded chemists.'

'There you are — you won't take a suggestion. You should have had half the force looking for him by now. He's tied up in this case more than anyone you've arrested.'

'What makes you think that?' said Sharkey.

'I'd rather not state that definitely right now. But I hope to be able to give you information about that thing he was working on shortly.'

'Okay,' Sharkey said. 'Call back then,

when you've got something definite to give us. The law needs something concrete before it can act.'

'It's *got* something concrete,' said Denby, walking towards the door, and looking directly at Sharkey's own head. He was halfway down the stairs before Sharkey, with a bull-like bellow, realised his implication . . .

★ ★ ★

There was a message for Denby on the call pad in his study. Miss Volt had copied it down, and it read: 'Professor Sylvester rang through. He wants you to see him as soon as you have time. Says he's analysed the notes you left. I'm going to bed now. Don't forget to wipe off any lipstick you may have picked up since last I saw you. Margery.'

His nerves tingling, Denby picked up the phone and asked for Sylvester's number. This was what he'd been waiting for. His half-formed suspicions would now be either crystallised as cold fact, or dismissed as fantastic fiction.

Sylvester said, 'Oh, it's you, Denby, my boy. Yes, I've found out something which may be rather startling. I'd prefer you to come round — much too big a thing to discuss over the phone. When? Now? Excellent. I'll wait up for you.'

Denby slapped down the receiver and reached for his hat.

★   ★   ★

'Sit down, my boy,' said Professor Sylvester, indicating a chair in the library, and seating himself at his desk. Denby sat down and sipped from the glass of whisky Sylvester had poured out for him.

The old professor fingered his silvery beard, then flipped the pages of Dr. Calthorp's notebook. He said at length, 'It took me quite a time to see what he was driving at, but finally I got it. At first it was too abnormal for my mind to grasp. I still find it hard to believe, but in view of these murders, and the strange absence of Calthorp, I *have* to believe it. It's the only solution. I mentioned before that there was a lot of data here about light rays, colour rays, refraction, reflection, absorption?'

'Yes, you told me that when I last saw you.'

'Hmm. Well, it puzzled me for some time to know what connection that information could have had to do with dyes. But after going through every one of the notes time after time, I suddenly knew what it was the doctor had stumbled upon — what so excited him, and why he vanished so completely.'

Denby tensed and sat forward. 'Yes?'

The professor said gravely, 'Dr. Calthorp, according to these notes, had stumbled upon the *secret of invisibility*!'

For a long interval neither man spoke again. Denby's mind was in a whirl, and the professor was giving him time to assimilate the statement. Finally Denby spoke first. 'I — I half-knew it was that,' he said softly. 'I've suspected it for days now. These murders had either to be supernatural, or else committed by a man no one else could see. And Calthorp had motive and means!'

'It very much looks like it,' agreed

Sylvester. 'In fact, it's the only reasonable way all the queer happenings lately can be explained away.'

'But I always understood Calthorp was a gentle sort of man. Can you tell me if this would affect his brain in any way?'

'Not unless the excitement did so. You see, Calthorp didn't have to take anything internally, if that's what you mean.'

'Then — how was it done?'

Sylvester flicked the notes again and leaned back. He put his fingertips together and scowled at the ceiling. 'I'll try to explain to you in non-technical language, Denby. Just how much you'll grasp I don't know. Firstly, Calthorp stumbled upon a dye with absolutely no absorptional strength. Possibly it didn't reflect light, or refract it either.

'He started to think what it would mean if he perfected his dye, so that it did not reflect or refract one solitary ray of light. And when he realised what it would mean, it must have awed even him for the moment. You see, everything you observe comes to you in waves — call them visional waves if you like. Now, while you look at my face, the view, although apparently solid enough, comes to your eyes across the room in waves, almost like rays of sunlight shining through a latticed window, only not so conspicuous.

'If a material was invented which could be inserted between your eyes and my face, and it was coloured with a dye which had no properties of refraction, reflection, or absorption, what would happen?' Denby shook his head. Sylvester said, 'What happens when you hold up your hand in a current of wind?'

'The wind bends round your hand and rejoins itself.'

'Exactly — and flows on as if your hand were not there at all. You have created a warp in the current. Now, assume the visional rays to be like a current of wind — and insert an object which won't do any of the normal things — like reflecting it, etcetera. What happens then?'

And all at once Denby grasped the enormity of it. He gasped. 'You mean — you mean the visional waves *would bend round it* — and come to your eyes?'

'Exactly. If a man had a suit dyed with

this substance — a single garment, say, which would cover him from head to foot — the waves of vision would simply bend themselves round him. Flow out into a warp, and come together again, like a stream of water when a stick is held upright in it. In other words, you would still see what, in the ordinary way, the man's body would be blocking from your view. The atmosphere would seem slightly distorted, but that wouldn't strike you. You'd attribute that to faulty vision.'

'I suspected that. But I'm damned if I don't still find it hard to believe. It's hardly possible for anyone to believe that a man could be . . . invisible.'

'It isn't as impossible as television would have been to any person alive in the sixteenth century. Suppose we put it this way. You know of the optical illusion, in which a black spot is brought forward on a card before your eyes until, when it is a certain distance from your pupil, you can no longer see it? That is what you call your blind spot, and it is an example of something you know is there, being completely invisible. Well, a man wearing a suit dyed with the dye Calthorp appears to have invented would be a continual blind spot to you. Understand?'

'I think I do. A sort of continual optical illusion?'

'Not quite, but it's as good a way of putting it as any.'

And then Denby remembered again the push he had felt on the edge of the ointment vat that very day, and the peculiar warp he had seen just above the iron ladder — and he knew beyond doubt that the professor was right, and that an invisible murderer was at large! He said, 'This is terrible, Sylvester. How the devil can we get the man before he kills anyone else?'

Sylvester shook his head and studied the ceiling again. 'The only way I can think of is to try to get a mark on the substance of his invisible garment in some way. A smear of paint would show up, for instance.'

'And he'd still be perfectly vulnerable to injury?'

'Certainly. He is only invisible — not dematerialised. Although we can't spot him, he'd be as solid as you or I.'

155

Denby lit a cigarette and gnawed the match with his teeth. The action reminded him sharply of Chief Inspector Sharkey and the vast machinery of the law. He said, 'How the dickens am I going to convince Sharkey there's an invisible man at large?'

'I'll come along to see him with you, my boy,' Sylvester told him. 'If we can't persuade him of the truth between us, he doesn't deserve to be on the force.'

'And there's Sheila, poor kid. What a terrible shock this will be for her.'

'Sheila?'

'Yes. Calthorp's daughter. As a matter of fact, I meant to ask her to marry me when all this mess had been cleared up. But now . . . '

'It is awkward,' Sylvester agreed.

'You see, she thinks her father's such a gentle old soul. She won't hear anything against him. She seemed quite sincere about him, too. It's hard to believe he's behind this shocking affair.'

'It is, I admit. But you know genius is next to madness, and when a meek sort of man suddenly finds himself with unlimited power, he often runs amok. Never mind, my boy; it will blow over sooner or later — and meanwhile, have another whisky!'

11

Terror at Large

Denby Collins and Professor Sylvester were shown into Chief Inspector Sharkey's office at the Yard early the following morning. Sharkey was seated behind the desk chewing a matchstick, a large pile of dossiers before him on the polished surface. He looked up as they entered and said, 'Sit down; be with you in a minute.'

'You'll be with us right now,' Denby told him. 'What we have to say is important. Do you imagine for one moment that anything less than a life-and-death matter could have got me out of bed at this ungodly hour, when only cats and policemen walk abroad?'

Sharkey sighed and pushed away the papers. He said, 'All right. You have the floor. Say on.'

'We've found out how these murders have been committed. All eight of them.

We can tell you just what to look for . . . '

Sharkey showed interest. He said, 'You aren't joking?'

'Never more serious, Inspector. It'll be a shock.'

'I can stand that. Tell me what I'm to look for,' said Sharkey, tilting back his chair and resting his crossed legs on the edge of the desk, 'if you really do know . . . ?'

'We do. Perhaps I shouldn't say 'look for' though. It's more a question of *finding* than looking.'

'Well go on, man, go on.'

'What you must find is — *an invisible man*!'

He had expected that statement to have a notable effect on the plump Yard man, and it did. His legs shot up in the air, his chair shot backwards, and he hit the floor with a thump and a howl. When they had helped him to his feet, he glared ferociously at them.

'If you think you can come in here and be funny, Collins, you're making a mistake. You can't make a fool of me, you know.'

'I know. It's too late. Tell him, Professor. Explain it all in words of one syllable so that his infantile brain can grasp it.'

Sylvester began to explain, quietly and convincingly. At the end of a quarter of an hour, Sharkey was won over by the matter-of-fact way the old professor spoke. He reached for the telephone and said into it, 'Put me on to the chief commissioner.'

In a few minutes Denby and the professor were repeating their story to the head man himself, and with the help of the diagrams which Sylvester had prepared he, too, was soon convinced.

Sharkey said, 'I think we can release the three suspects in view of this, can't we, sir?'

'It would be as well; we don't wish to detain anyone who may be innocent. But you could still have them watched. Mr. Sharkey, get a dragnet out for this murderer. Scour the city. I know it's awkward looking for something you can't see, but we'll have to make a move of some sort until he takes it into his head to show his hand again.'

Sharkey nodded and left the office. Denby and Sylvester stayed with him as he put the entire power of the Metropolitan force into looking for an invisible man. Then they accompanied him to the cells, where the three suspects were temporarily located.

'We're letting them out,' Sharkey told the desk sergeant. They cut through a green door at the back of the room and down a short passage. In the first two cells they found Arnolds, the valet, and Dr. Moss. They were released and told to wait in the other room. They went on down to the end cell where Burnham had been placed the previous night. Sharkey fitted the key and swung the door. Lester Buraham was lying on a narrow bench at the far end of the small cell, stomach downwards.

Sharkey said, 'Get up, Burnham. We're turning you loose.'

Burnham didn't move. Sharkey said more loudly, 'Hey, Burnham! Get up. You're sprung.' He grunted irritably and shook the recumbent man by the shoulder, then turned him over onto his back.

Burnham's head lolled back fantastically and Sharkey gave a start. He made a quick examination, then turned to face the others. He said, 'This is one who *doesn't* get home again — his neck's been snapped like a stalk of celery!'

'But if he's been locked in here all the time, how . . . ?'

The desk sergeant said, 'There hasn't been anyone in to see him since he arrived, except the lawyer he phoned. He came early this morning.'

Sylvester gasped. 'Then that's it — that's how it was done! Don't you see? When the lawyer came, the invisible man was hanging about, waiting for his chance to kill Burnham. I don't know why he would want to do that, but if he had a grievance against Burnham's lady friend, it's also quite likely he extended it to Burnham as well. When the lawyer was admitted he went in, too, waited until the lawyer left, then suddenly got a grip on Burnham and snapped his throat!'

'But how the devil did he get out again?'

'He couldn't have done that after the lawyer left, unless . . . unless the door has been opened.'

'It hasn't been opened since then, sir,' the sergeant told them.

Sylvester said quietly and calmly, 'You realise what that means, gentlemen? That Calthorp *must* have been in this cell when we opened the door! And since Denby and I have been blocking the exit, he can't have left yet! In fact, *he's still here!*'

And as if to verify his words, the cell suddenly echoed with the sound of half-mad, mocking laughter.

Sharkey said, 'Good God, he *is* here! Calthorp — wherever you are, give yourself up now, or . . . ' His words were suddenly cut short. He doubled up in pain, and the wind escaped from his lungs in a gusty hiss. There was a second peal of demented laughter, and then Sharkey's feet suddenly left the ground, rose into the air, and flung the inspector backwards, his head connecting nastily with the end of the wooden bench.

Denby said, 'Quick — shut the cell door!'

The thought was too late, for even as they began to put it into effect, something smacked into their chests with the force of a battering ram, and they were hurled backwards. And then they distinctly heard the soft sound of pattering feet retreating down the corridor.

The door at the far end was whipped open, then slammed to again. The invisible Calthorp had gone.

Sylvester was first on his feet, and without pausing he raced down towards the door, opened it, and yelled to the astonished constables in the room: 'Lock the door — lock it, you fools, quickly!'

The men stared at him blankly, and Sylvester rushed across to the far door himself, seized the bolts to ram them home, and then stood there hoping to prevent the invisible man's escape.

A chair suddenly rose from one corner and floated across the air to within a yard of him. He watched, fascinated; it swung high, and Sylvester ducked, but the chair followed his movement and crashed down on his head with sickening force.

But Denby Collins and Sharkey were in play again now; they both rushed over to the door, Sharkey hurling commands to his men. The desk sergeant hurried up with the key, and the door was locked.

The constables there drew truncheons and prepared to give the unseen quantity a taste of English wood. Sharkey bawled, 'Line the room and close in towards the centre. Speed it up.'

They began to move in towards the centre of the room, making vigorous but futile swipes with their truncheons. The foremost gaped as his truncheon was suddenly wrenched from his hand, his helmet pushed off, and the stick brought down on his bared head. There was another burst of laughter from the murderer, and then the truncheon hurled itself at the nearest constable, and the whereabouts of the fugitive was in doubt again.

A paperweight picked itself up off the desk as they stood gaping; it flew straight and true through the air, billeting on Sharkey's already aching head. He groaned with pain. A voice called, 'You poor, helpless fools! Do you think you can catch me? *Me?* No one can catch me — I am the master of you all! Single-handed I could fight an army.' The voice was high, vibrant, charged with the erratic personality of its owner. It went on, 'I wondered how long it would take you idiots to learn the truth. But even now you have learned it, it will be of no use to you. I can never be taken, *never!*'

'That's your opinion,' said Sharkey grimly. 'But you're as good as taken already. You can't get out of this room, you know that.'

'I can't? Why, my fat, flaccid, flat-footed friend, I can leave here any moment I desire to do so.'

The door leading to the cells suddenly crashed open. Sharkey yelled, 'He's trapped himself in that passage! You men get after him — it's a dead end, and you're bound to get him. Search each cell as you come to it.'

The intrepid constabulary poured themselves through the door to the last man. Arnolds and Dr. Moss, excited by the chase, went with them. Denby and Sharkey remained at the door.

No sooner had the last constable left the room, than the door to the cells slammed shut again for no apparent reason. The key, which was in the lock, suddenly twisted. They were locked in. Then the key left the keyhole, dangled in air for a second, and completely vanished!

'Now, my friends,' came the voice of the invisible man, softly, 'You are confident I cannot escape from this room? I have disposed of the others by a neat little ruse. There remains only you two . . . and you, Inspector, have the key!'

Sharkey said, 'And I'm sticking to it.'

'Really? How foolish of you to think so, Inspector. You are well aware that at any given moment I could kill either one — or both — of you. I advise you to throw that key in the centre of the floor, and stand clear of the door.'

'You can go to hell.'

The invisible man sighed and said, 'Someday, no doubt. But unless you either surrender the key or open the door for me, at once, I will be compelled to add another assault to my already numerous score.'

Denby, speaking for the first time, said: 'Calthorp — what's got into you? Why are you committing all these murders?'

'Reasons. I have reasons. Of course, it is not my wish to kill anyone against whom I have no grievance. You gentlemen, for example, will be perfectly safe if you do as I say. Will you produce that key?'

Sharkey made a sudden grab for the chair by the door and swung it aloft threateningly. He said, 'One move from you, and I'll use this where it'll do most good.'

Then, to his amazement, the chair was snatched from his grip and thrown across the room. An invisible fist smote him violently in the chin, a second fist impinged with some velocity on his right ear, and to the helpless inspector the world seemed to suddenly become a nightmare of unseen hammer-like blows. Sharkey lashed out himself valiantly, and once or twice succeeded in landing a punch on his attacker; but his blows did no harm, and a terrific jolt to the chin suddenly put the stout policeman completely out of action.

Denby Collins came in, fists flying, striking at a distorted patch of air before him. His guess was accurate, and there were three grunts from the invisible man as his fists found their mark three times. Then Denby felt a foot smack home into his groin and he doubled up, gasping with agony.

'I warned you,' sneered the invisible man. 'But you would insist on being the little heroes. Ah, well.' He bent over Sharkey, rummaging through his pockets for the key, and said, 'I intend to take the key to the door on which your trapped constables are so frantically hammering. I regret it will cause some inconvenience, but doubtless they will survive.'

He unlocked the outer door as Denby began to uncurl from his rolled-up position. Denby watched, unable to rise, as a carafe of water floated over the room and emptied itself upon the unconscious Sharkey. It was the invisible man's parting shot. Then the outer door slammed and the murderer departed, carrying with him the two keys.

* * *

'Invisible man?' said Miss Volt, patting her blonde locks into position at the nape of her neck. 'Good heavens! A girl couldn't have any privacy if ever the secret became universal property. I expect *you*,' she added scathingly to Denby, 'would buy a suit immediately! You'd love it, wouldn't you?'

'I rather think it would be interesting,' he agreed, his eyes twinkling. 'Yes, even fascinating.'

'You wolf,' snorted Miss Volt. 'You sheep in wolves' clothing. You peeping Tom, you!'

'Peeping Tom, eh? And you, my dear Miss Volt, would have the honour of being my first Lady Godiva.'

'Sorry,' said Miss Volt, 'I haven't got either the hair or the horse for it.'

'I'd settle for a pony,' Denby told her.

He was at his apartments, waiting for a call from Sheila Calthorp, whom he had not seen since the startling news Sylvester had given him. Actually he was a little worried as to how he would inform her

170

about her father; it promised to be a painful job, and one that he wouldn't relish in any way. He had become very fond of the girl, and to have to hurt her was going to be hard. Nevertheless, he thought it would be better for her to hear it from him, gently, than to hear it on the news or read about it in the newspapers.

Miss Volt had tried to get Sheila's home on the phone three or four times. So far she had failed; it seemed that Sheila must be out for the afternoon. Denby hoped she would ring him up when she returned. He said, 'Skipping the Lady Godiva business for the moment, Miss Volt, how about trying that number again?'

Miss Volt sniffed and nodded. After a long wait she put down the phone again with a 'Thank you.'

'Any luck?'

'Yewa numba dessn't onsa,' mimicked Miss Volt.

Denby cursed under his breath, drawing a shocked gaze from his secretary. He stood up and said, 'If anyone calls, you can get in touch with me at Sheila

Calthorp's. I'll go along and wait for her down there.'

'Wait? But how can you get in if she's out? You'd look sillier than you normally do standing on the doorstep, perhaps for hours on end.'

'I sometimes wonder,' he told her, 'why I ever tolerate you. I should be entitled to *some* respect, at least. Why on earth do I put up with you at all?'

She said, 'Perhaps it's because I know too much about you. Or perhaps it's simply because I have a knack for getting you out of those jams you get into with women. Then, again, it might be just that you like beautiful women about.'

'Then why don't I fire you and get one?' suggested Denby, and she glared at him. He grinned and said, 'Maybe it's because you *are* a good secretary. We'll let it go at that.'

She said darkly, 'We'd better — before I resign.'

He left her typing out some notes for his next book, donned coat and gloves, phoned a cab, and was whisked over town to Sheila's home. He knocked at the door and received no answer. His eyes suddenly fastened on the morning milk which stood on the step, and on the previous evening's paper, folded and pushed half through the letter box. That meant that Sheila must have left the house again soon after she had gone home, after leaving him. Or had she gone home at all? He had told her he'd get in touch with her, and she had said she would stay in and wait for his call. Strange that she shouldn't have been home all night.

He decided something was very wrong and started to walk round the place, examining each window to see if it were fastened. Reaching the back, he tried the rear door. Locked. He found the kitchen window and peered through. Taking his penknife from his pocket, he slid it inside, experiencing no difficulty in dislodging the catch. He pushed the frame up, got one leg on the sill, and eased himself through until he was standing in the sink. He jumped down and moved into the house.

In the sitting room the reading lamp

was burning, and by the side of it lay an opened novel. Denby grunted and began to search the bungalow from top to bottom. Half an hour later he was forced to admit to himself that Sheila Calthorp had vanished entirely, leaving no trace of where, or why, she had gone!

12

The Unseen Bandit

Mr. Frost-Thomson, manager of the London City branch of the Holdsworth's City and Suburban Bank, relaxed behind his desk and felt in his hip pocket. Despite his meek and mild appearance, he was somewhat addicted to that which the vulgar term 'the bottle' applied, but which he preferred to look on as his 'medicine'. As medicine it had its points — but hardly in the quantities Mr. F-T liked to imbibe it. He canted the half-pint flask to his lips and issued a happy sigh as the nectar flowed down his throat, warming him with subtle fires.

His already red nose glowed like a beacon; his breath fairly sizzled the atmosphere. He delicately put the flask away, took from his pocket three scented cachous, and popped them into his mouth. He sucked them thoughtfully;

then, cupping his hands round his mouth, breathed into them, and quickly sniffed up. Satisfied that no trace of odour remained, he turned his attention to his work again. For the next half hour he rifled through the stacks of ten-pound notes on his desk; then he broke off for a further swig of his life-restorer.

It was just after he had finished his three regulation cachous that he was alarmed by the sound of the door behind him closing softly. He whizzed round, the grim thought that the president had sneaked in unexpectedly to catch him drinking uppermost in his mind. To his surprise the door was closed; not a soul was in the room.

Mr. Frost-Thomson was puzzled. He inserted a little finger in either ear and twiddled; he pursed his lips. Then he dipped into his flask again and helped himself to a further liberal sample of the right stuff. He smacked his lips with gusto, ran his tongue about them, and re-corked the devil's brew. He sucked more cachous.

It was at this precise moment that the chair he was sitting on, for some inexplicable reason, swayed backward and tipped him onto the unsympathetic floor. This dazed him; he sat there, blinking, uncertain what steps to take with a rebellious chair. He was quite certain that he had not caused the mishap himself. He looked searchingly at the chair legs, but there was no sign of them being weak or broken.

Unnerved, he replaced the chair and sat himself at his desk once more. Then his eyes glued to the money he had been working on. For three of the eight stacks of notes had neatly vanished! Three thousand pounds!

Mr. Frost-Thomson's head buzzed. It wasn't possible! He knelt down and began to search the floor, thinking that possibly the notes had fallen there. He was nicely positioned for a kick, had there been anyone there to deliver it. But he knew quite well there was not.

Nevertheless, he received the kick!

Mr. Frost-Thomson shot forward with a wild exclamation of surprise. He scrambled hastily to his feet and turned like the stag at bay. He had been attacked.

His dignity had been sullied. Someone would pay for the outrage. Some practical joker. He would be dismissed at once, and forbidden to ever darken Mr. Frost-Thomson's bank doors again.

So thought the manager; but to his wrathful and enquiring eyes there appeared only empty space. No one was in the room.

And now, where there had been five stacks of notes remaining on the desk, there were only two!

He goggled and wondered if he was going mad, but worse was yet to come. For before his eyes, yet another stack was wafted into the air and immediately became non-existent. It vanished.

The last stack began to move, and with a desperate rush the manager plunged to the desk and slapped his hand down upon it. He felt a tug, and the notes slid from under his fingers and followed the other seven stacks. For some minutes Mr. Frost-Thomson stared stonily at the empty desk. Then he looked round to see if any windows were open, any draughts blowing into the room.

The windows were all shut.

He collapsed limply into his chair. He could not believe his eyes. It was too much.

Hallucinations. Overwork. He must have been working too hard. His gaze was suddenly turned on the door — he had seen the door handle move. From that direction came a thin and mocking voice.

'I'm sorry I can't leave you a receipt, my friend.'

The door opened; the door shut. No one had gone out or come in, and no one was near that door.

The manager gave a muffled groan and put his head in his hands. His doctor had warned him about this . . .

With sudden resolution he left his seat, walked over to one of the windows and opened it. He took his flask from his hip pocket and cast it into the convenient dustbin beneath. Drinking was all right, thought Mr. Frost-Thomson; but when a man starts getting delirium tremens . . .

That done, he got on his hands and knees and began scouring the floor for the elusive money. He didn't find it for the simple reason that it was now progressing down the busy Strand, tucked beneath the garment of an invisible man!

* * *

The wage clerk from Modern Stores Ltd. tucked the old valise firmly under his arm and took a short cut through a narrow entry. As he walked he mused on the possible results of anyone being aware of just how much that bag contained. Twenty thousand pounds in various notes. And here he was, carrying it through the streets in a dilapidated valise. No one, of course, would expect to find it in there. Unless someone at the bank had seen it being loaded into the bag — and that was impossible, since only the clerk had been in the bank at that particular moment.

He had almost reached the end of the deserted entry, when his neck was seized by some invisible force. His head was whacked with great vigour against the wall, and he sank to the floor unconscious.

When a passer-by found him five minutes later, the valise lay by his side — but now it was devoid of anything but its tattered lining!

★   ★   ★

The croupier at Dan's Select Gambling Saloon, which operated — unknown to the police — in a shabby district of Limehouse, spun the wheel with accustomed dexterity and sang out, 'Place your stakes, ladies and gentlemen!'

The money on the board grew thickly; the croupier decided the house should have the rake-off this time. He fumbled under the table, counted along a row of what seemed to be ordinary screw heads, and pressed the tenth. No bets were on ten. A powerful magnet came into operation, and the clacking ball jerked suddenly into ten and stayed there.

'Dix,' said the croupier, airing his scanty knowledge of French in the hope that Dan's fashionable patrons would think he hailed from that intriguing country. The ball, to his surprise, suddenly whizzed from ten of its own volition and lodged in twenty-one.

'Er, hell — I mean, Vingt-et-un,' he stammered.

But apparently the ball was not yet satisfied with its accommodation. It rose again abruptly, shot through the air, and landed in number three. The croupier gaped foolishly and said, 'Trois.'

The ball took another short flight to five. This time the croupier forgot himself and said, 'What the hell . . . ?'

He leaned forward to fix his eyes on the errant ball, and it suddenly rose up and hit him forcibly in the left eye. He gasped.

A tall, burly man, by his accent an American, snarled, 'This damn game's rigged. He's doing that himself — I seen it back home in the States. The whole goddam thing's a fake!'

The croupier, rubbing his eye, expostulated feebly; the angry crowd round the table glared at him murderously. They were inclined to believe the American gentleman, for the ball could not possibly have been so eccentric without the influence of hidden magnets.

The croupier was just wondering how he was going to get out of the scrape, when a woman screamed, 'My God! Look!'

The piles of notes on the table (Dan's didn't issue counters; you played with cash) had begun to slide towards one blank corner. The burly American was the first to realise what was happening. He bawled, 'There's some damned trickery here,' and made a great leap to the corner. His hands reached for the notes, but before he could secure them, a most astonishing thing happened. His feet jerked from under him, and he dented the table with his prominent nose.

Simultaneously a stool was picked up, and threw itself at the lights above, smashing them and plunging the room into darkness. Above the terrified shrieks of women came a malicious, triumphant laugh.

By the time someone had the presence of mind to use his torch, the money had completely vanished.

★ ★ ★

183

'And how the devil,' said Chief Inspector Sharkey wearily, 'are we going to catch a man we can't even see?'

Professor Sylvester, his head bandaged where the chair had struck it two days previously, said, 'There's only one way to expose the man — by marking him in some way.'

'Is that all?' said Sharkey sarcastically. 'Oh well, that's child's play. I'll walk round with a can of red paint until he comes up to me and says, 'I'm the chap you're looking for — just put a dab or two on my back so you'll know where I am, will you, old bean?'

Sylvester smiled at the inspector's irritation and looked at Denby Collins. He said, 'I think perhaps Mr. Collins has an idea.'

Denby Collins nodded. 'I have an idea that's well worth a trial,' he explained. 'My theory is that wherever our man is, he has Miss Calthorp with him. It's hardly likely to turn out that she is an accessory to the murders and thefts her father is committing, so for some reason he must be holding her prisoner against her will. Now, if he thought his hideout was going to be found, he'd have to move the girl, and that would be damned awkward for an invisible man. The more likely thing would be for him to stop the place being found if he could. He'd murder to do that. Before I go any further, I'd like you to meet Madam Acanti.' He stepped to the office door, opened it, and admitted a thin, self-possessed looking female of middle age, and with the looks and manners of a Sunday-school teacher.

Sharkey said, 'What the devil has she to do with it?'

'The madam is London's most noted spiritualist — isn't that so?'

'It is,' agreed Sharkey. 'So noted that we've had her in court once or twice. But . . . where does she come in?'

'That's my plan,' smiled Denby. 'And I'm certain that if you assured the madam the hounds of the law wouldn't bother her in the future, she'd be willing to co-operate with us. Would you not, Madam Acanti?'

'Would I? Rather. I'd co-operate in

anything — within reason of course — to prevent those nosey policemen spying on me.'

'Exactly. You see, Sharkey, we'll have a séance. The madam will do her stuff, and will get in touch with the spirits of the people the invisible man's murdered. They'll tell us where to find the chap.'

Sharkey spilled a box of matches in his emotion and said, 'Are you *completely* crazy, Collins? Why, the woman can't get in touch with any spirits — she's a *charlatan!*'

''ere,' said Madam Acanti aggrievedly. 'I'm no such thing. I was born and bred a Protestant, and I go to church regular.'

'Ignore the inspector,' Denby told her. 'He talks too much before he knows what he's talking about. You haven't heard the rest of it yet, Sharkey.'

'Go on then, let's hear it.'

'It's quite simple. We'll have it broadcast, and published in the newspapers on the front page, that Scotland Yard have been convinced Madam Acanti can get in touch with the spirits of the murderer's victims, and that they are attending a séance to question them as to where and how the killer can be picked up. Calthorp will see it, and will take no chances. He'll be at that séance, just in case . . . '

'You think he will?'

'Sure of it. And if he thinks the madam is going to reveal anything, he'll kill her!'

Madam Acanti began to walk rapidly towards the door. Sylvester said, 'Where are you going, Madam Acanti?'

'I'm not going to be killed,' she stated firmly. 'And that's a fact. You didn't say nothing about nobody being killed, you didn't. It isn't good enough. I'm going.'

Sharkey, who had begun to see possibilities in the idea, said, 'You'll be protected, Madam. Don't be afraid. I'll see to that.'

The madam stopped, considered, and returned. Sharkey continued, 'In addition we'll see you get a nice little reward. Done?'

'Done. But if I'm killed in spite of you, there'll be a row, you mark my words.'

Sharkey smiled. 'There's only one thing,' he said. 'The media will make us look awful fools about this. It won't have to be official. For the sake of having a chance to trap the man, I'll let them use my name in conjunction with the story. But there must be no mention of the Yard itself having sanctioned the performance.'

'That would do nicely,' Denby said.

'Another thing — if we do get the devil in the room, how will we know? How can we trap him even then?'

'That's Sylvester's department. He'll explain that.'

'That's the simplest part of the plan. The room in which the madam holds her sittings can be reached only through an archway over which hang curtains. The house will be kept locked every minute when the story is published, right up to the time when we walk in for the séance. The front door will be left slightly open then.

'The second we are in the actual room in which the séance will take place, I will switch on a little device which has already been fitted up in the madam's home. It consists of an electric spray which will be filled with white paint and a, er, new perfume I have recently perfected. The moment anyone steps on the mat beyond

188

the archway, the spray will automatically operate and shoot a screen of white paint and scent — rather strong scent — onto anyone entering the room. The paint will cling to the invisible man's garment; the scent will serve to give his position away if he breaks out into the shrubbery. One way and another, if you take care to have the place surrounded by concealed men, we will catch the invisible man!'

Sharkey's eyes were gleaming. He said, 'I see it now. The paint will stick to him and show us just where he is. I — I half think it might work, if the man only comes.'

'He'll come, I think,' said Denby. 'Already his conscience must be haunted by those he's killed. And anyway, he thinks he is invincible.'

Sharkey reached for the telephone and started issuing orders. The plan was rapidly put into operation.

* * *

The headlines of the *Daily Banner* and most other London newspapers were startling in the extreme that night. The *Banner* had treated the subject humorously, welcoming the chance of a sly dig at Chief Inspector Sharkey. The story read:

'AMUSING TURN OF EVENTS IN INVISIBLE MAN CASE. SCOTLAND YARD MAN CALLS IN SPIRITS. Earlier today, Chief Inspector Sharkey — handling the case of the Invisible Murderer — informed our reporter that it is his intention to hold a séance at the home of Madam Acanti tonight. The madam, who is not unknown to the police, believes she can contact the souls of the invisible man's victims, and from them find out where he can be discovered. This seems rather strange to us, since it is not two weeks since the madam was on trial for trickery and extortion of money under false pretences. However, we are assured that the madam truly believes she can locate the murderer, and evidently Chief Inspector Sharkey agrees with her. We wish them luck, but we respectfully venture the opinion that possibly Chief Inspector Sharkey has been in close contact with spirits *other* than those of Madam Acanti's!'

This opinion made Sharkey fume and made another gentleman, the subject of the séance, purse his lips thoughtfully . . .

13

The Last Victim

The outer districts of London's East End were strangely silent the night of the séance. Eager sightseers continually thronged the pavement in the vicinity of Madam Acanti's home and were impatiently moved along by the police. It would spoil everything if the surroundings of the house were crowded; the invisible killer might not care to chance attempting anything.

The throngs were finally dispersed with the threat of arrest for obstructing the police, and the immediate neighbourhood was cleared. The constables took up their positions in the shrubbery early, and remained under cover.

At eight minutes past ten a police car drew up. From it stepped Chief Inspector Sharkey, Denby Collins, and Professor Sylvester. They proceeded along the short path to Madam Acanti's door, and knocked.

The madam, who had remained locked in all day, called: 'Is that you, Inspector?'

Sharkey reassured her, and she opened the door and admitted them. The door was then left partially ajar.

Two minutes passed, and then there was a sudden slight rustle in the shrubbery bordering the pathway. A loose stone just before the front door stirred. The door opened yet further!

Inside the house, the madam was regaling her visitors with a cup of tea before the session took place. She wore a plain black gown with a high throat line, and her severe features were more so than ever. Clearly the madam regarded this business as being of deadly importance — possibly she even hoped to really contact the spirits.

'Now,' said the madam, at length, 'I think we will repair to the other room, gentlemen.'

She unlocked a door leading to a passage, and they went through. Walking so that no one could pass them, they moved towards the arch leading into the rear room. The moment they had entered,

Sylvester moved quickly and flipped a small lever hidden behind the nearest drapes. The four looked at each other, and Chief Inspector Sharkey smiled and nodded imperceptibly.

The stage was set, and the spray switched on. The invisible man could hardly be in the room; he still had to come, if he was coming at all. And the second he passed over the rug just inside the archway, the spray would shower him with strongly scented white paint.

The madam indicated a small round table covered by a black cloth. They seated themselves in the prepared positions, Sharkey facing the door. The medium flipped the light switches and the white garish electric globes were cut out, giving way to green, mystical lighting from concealed niches in the walls. Certainly the madam gave her clients their money's worth.

She seated herself at the head of the table, her back to the door, and said, 'Please join hands. Place your fingers flat on the table, and permit the tips of the little fingers to touch.' They obeyed, every eye watchful and alert. She continued, 'The object of this séance is to discover the whereabouts of the man responsible for murdering nine people recently. To that end we shall endeavour to contact the spirits.'

'I'd like to contact the spirits in a Johnnie Walker bottle just at the moment,' whispered Denby.

'Silence!' hissed Madam Acanti. 'There must be no levity. You must believe — you must think hard of the dear departed. No matter what I do or say, you must not do anything which will disturb me. That would be dangerous.'

She was really losing herself in her performance now. Her face contorted into a mask of wrinkles. She stiffened in her chair and drew upright. Her eyes closed.

'Madam,' whispered Sharkey, 'are you all right?'

She opened one eye and winked at him. Then she said in a deep, sonorous voice, 'The spirits are violent tonight. They fight to speak through my lips. They fight . . . ' A wild tremor shook her body and spluttering noises left her lips. Her jaws opened mechanically. She said, 'I am here — ask what you will of me.'

Sharkey, following the pre-arranged plan, said, 'Who are you?'

'I am the spirit of Angela Taylor. I was murdered at my flat.'

'Can you tell us where we can locate the man who killed you?'

'I can tell . . . *eeeeeh!*'

It was a terrible, sobbing shriek. Madam Acanti stopped her act and slumped forward across the table. The others could see the handle of the ugly knife which had been thrown unerringly into her back on the heart line!

And from just beyond the archway, a maniacal laugh broke into the sudden stillness. A voice said, 'You fools! I am not to be tricked so easily. I am interested in your activities, and by a lucky chance I was actually in the office at the Yard when you evolved this plan. I determined to show you your plan would not work, and still kill the woman. It will serve as a warning! It will pay you to remember that I am invincible!'

And then Denby Collins jerked his revolver up and sent three bullets spinning towards the archway!

There was a strangled cry. The three men surged towards the archway, Sharkey first. And as his foot touched the rug, the white paint mixed with scent showered him from head to foot!

Denby and Sylvester didn't feel much like laughing then; it was an incident they could save up to recite in their clubs later. But the shower expended, they rushed through and down the hall.

Sylvester said, 'He may have gone upstairs. I'll try there. You slip out and warn the policemen he's at large somewhere.'

Denby nodded and, joined by Sharkey who had rushed up, a mass of white paint, they broke from the house and towards the shrubbery. There was a sudden yell and three constables burst from cover, hurled themselves upon Sharkey, and used their truncheons with some power upon his form. Sharkey howled.

'You idiots,' gasped Denby. 'That's the inspector. The man we want didn't enter the room to get the benefit of the spray, but he's somewhere near here, and I think he's wounded.' The men grasped the situation and, leaving the dazed Sharkey to stagger on his own, they played tunes on their whistles.

Denby cut through the bushes towards the gate. He came across one or two hurrying constables, but no sign of any unaccountable movement in the foliage. But as he reached the gate he saw what was happening near the police car, parked slightly along the road.

The driver was standing by the rear mudguard, staring towards the house whence came the blast of the whistles. He had been in the act of looking for something in the open boot. Then, behind him, a large stone had raised itself in the air!

Even as Denby opened his lips to shout, it crashed down, throwing the man to the ground. The car door opened and shut; the self-starter was pressed. Denby arrived just as the car gathered power and shot down the road. He lodged himself inside the open boot and hung on. The driverless car roared into the night, ignoring traffic signals and policemen on point duty alike.

It was a nightmare journey for Denby. All he was aware of was the sensation of rushing power, and the cramping of his limbs as he clung for life. That, and the gaping faces of the startled pedestrians they whirled past. He had to hope that in his agitation to escape, the driver was unaware that the boot was open or, even if he were, he was unaware that Denby had hurled himself inside.

They were out of the busy streets, tearing along the road that Denby remembered as leading to Dr. Calthorp's home. Here it was quieter, and the car jerked to a halt before the bungalow. The door opened and shut again; the killer had left the car. But to Denby's surprise, the gate leading to the bungalow did not open. Following the slamming of the car door there was absolute silence.

Denby slid from the boot and looked cautiously round the car. Was the invisible man there, or had he continued his flight?

The writer's eyes fell upon a red stain,

plainly revealed by the moonlight.

Blood! From the wound he had inflicted on the killer!

He came out into the open, and now he could see there was a trail of spots. He followed them along the pavement, across the road. They occurred intermittently for about a hundred yards, then suddenly stopped.

He retraced his steps to the last one and went in at the gate opposite. The house which confronted him was of a type similar to the doctor's home — the same squat half-rustic bungalow with mullioned windows. The blood spots ran right up to the front door, which was ajar. Cautiously he opened it further and, nothing happening, he eased silently into the dark passage. There was a room door at the far end of this, and from behind it came sounds of life. He tiptoed along until he had reached it, bent, and applied his eye to the keyhole.

There were two people in the room: Sheila Calthorp and a grey-haired, distinguished-looking gentleman of mature years. They were both bound at the wrists, their bonds being fastened to iron staples driven into the woodwork. They were talking together, but Denby could not hear what they said.

He tried the door. Locked. He took a chance, drew his gun from his pocket, and discharged bullets into the lock. He waited a minute, ready to face the invisible man should the shots bring him. Then he burst into the room.

The girl gave a glad cry as she realised it was Denby, and he commenced to untie her without any further arguments. That done, he started unfastening the man's bonds while Sheila massaged the circulation back into her wrists. The man looked as if he had been kept prisoner for some days. There was deep stubble on his chin, and his features were lined and worried.

When they were both unfastened, Denby said, 'I'm glad I got here. But who's your companion in distress, Sheila?'

'Why, that's my father! Father, this is Mr. Collins — Denby Collins.'

The man said, 'I'm glad you came along, young man. I don't know what would have happened to Sheila if you hadn't . . . '

'But if *this* is Dr. Calthorp, who is the

invisible man?' stammered Denby.

Before Calthorp could reply, there was a fresh development. The revolver which Denby had laid aside while he untied the two was snatched into air. A mocking voice said, '*I* am, Mr. Collins! Keep perfectly still, or I shoot.'

'Who — who the devil are *you*?' snapped Denby, peering towards the gun which pointed at them unwaveringly.

'I think you've met me. My name is *Street* — *Jack Street!* Remember? I believe we met at the flat of my late fiancée, did we not?'

'*Street!* But what . . . ?'

The invisible man moved slightly but kept his gun steady. A decanter of brandy on the table near the gun suddenly tilted into a glass there. The glass raised itself in the air, tilted, and the liquid trickled out to vanish.

'I needed that,' said the invisible man calmly. 'Your shot grazed my right cheek, Mr. Collins. A nasty wound, I think. It's bled quite a lot, and also it ripped the cloth of my invisible garment.'

Denby noticed for the first time a dull

red splotch in the air at about the height of a man's cheek. Blood was dripping from this every so often, and falling onto the floor in a crimson pool.

The invisible man went on, 'However, it is only superficial, and nothing to be alarmed about. I'm not sure if you are entitled to an explanation before I kill you, but you shall have one. After all, it will satisfy my vanity to give it, and to let you know what I plan to do with my invisibility next.

'I know you suspected Calthorp — and that is precisely what I hoped you would do. The story dates back to the time when I worked in the same laboratory as Calthorp, at Public Promotions. I knew then he was trying to solve the secret of invisibility, and we came to an arrangement by which, if he was lucky, we would exploit the discovery together without handing it over to the firm, who had already cheated him once.

'Soon after that I was dismissed for incompetence. That made things rather awkward for me. The dismissal had been in the shape of a request for my resignation, and although it was not generally known I was actually *told* to go, the board of directors refused me a testimonial or reference. I couldn't get work anywhere, for jobs were scarce even for competent men like Calthorp, let alone fledglings like myself. My misery was aggravated by the fact that my unemployed condition prevented me from marrying the girl I was in love with — the late, unlamented Angela Taylor, whom I killed.

'It was awkward all round, you see; and when I saw that Angela was beginning to get tired of me, I attributed it all to the six directors and the general manager of the firm, who had reported me. At the time I had made an appeal against dismissal to the board of directors. They put it to the common vote in my presence, and every one of them voted I should be asked to tender my resignation. They did nasty things in a nice way, Mr. Collins.

'You will understand how bitter I became, and how my anger against them grew when Angela started to make attempts to get rid of me. And then, one night, Dr. Calthorp arrived at this house. He arrived without my knowledge, and almost made me jump from my skin when he spoke beside my very ear.

'Finally I knew all. He had discovered the dye which would so treat a material that visional waves would flow round it and would thus make the cloth invisible. He had gone further than that, by dyeing a one-piece costume in wool — carefully fashioned with tiny eye-slits so the wearer could see out — which he had had made in readiness, drying it in his oven, and donning it himself to come along and show me. When he told me he would have to get back as his daughter did not even know he had left the house yet, my scheme began to shape itself at once.

'The doctor had seated himself in a chair directly opposite me, and was looking at me directly. I could see his eyes! So it was an easy matter to locate him and knock the doctor senseless and tie him up in here. I did just that. Then I availed myself of his suit. I soon realised that I would be invisible to any onlooker just so long as I did not look into their eyes directly, and as my first experiment I chose Señor Ventura, whom I despised more than the rest.

'After that all went, shall I say, swimmingly. I wandered about at will, murdering whom, when and where I liked. In a few short days I had struck terror into the hearts of the men I loathed so much — and not only terror, but death! One by one I saw them die, and chuckled at the amazement caused by their deaths. But something happened for which I had not bargained.

'That something was in the shape of Miss Calthorp here. A very admirable shape I admit, but nevertheless troublesome. It was after I had left you with Angela, Mr. Collins. I was returning home to get into my invisible garment again, for I was angry, and decided that Angela must die for her unfaithfulness. I was aware she had been having an affair behind my back with Burnham — and with the directors and the manager out of the way, I could now turn my attention to other people I detested. For I really did detest her now, and I had no need of her.

With the money I could accumulate in my unseen state, I could have my pick of women.

'I had rushed into the garden path when I became aware that Sheila, here, was standing on the porch. She knew that her father and I were good friends, or had been, but she did not know of our plan to exploit his inventions together. If she had done so, she might have guessed earlier what had taken place. I asked her in, thinking she had merely come to enquire about her father. She had, and I denied having seen him for at least six months. Then she showed me a note which she had found beneath the sink in his laboratory. She said she had been sweeping up, and had thought it was some of his data at first, but after she had read it . . .

'It was a letter, actually — a few lines scribbled on paper, in which Calthorp told her not to be alarmed at his absence; that he had slipped along to my home on important business and would be back as soon as possible. He also mentioned his discovery of the secret of invisibility. It seems the note had been left on the bench, and must have been blown under the sink by the draught from the door when he had left the lab in his invisible suit.

'Naturally I again denied having seen him, which was foolish because she had noticed a cigarette in the ashtray which bore the name of a somewhat rare brand which the doctor has sent to him from Egypt. This was as good as conclusive proof that I *had* seen him, and she was silly enough to tax me directly with it. In the circumstances there was only one thing to do. That was to hold her along with her father. Which I did.

'Then I returned and murdered Angela; and later I killed off Burnham in the cell. I should have killed him earlier, but I wanted him to suffer mentally before the end. As he probably did. And the rest, I think, you should be able to guess.'

The invisible man finished speaking in a dead silence. Then Denby said, 'There's just one point I'm not too clear on: why didn't you murder Calthorp and get rid of the body? Why leave him alive when he was a potential danger? The same applies to Sheila.'

'That was part of my plan. I knew that sooner or later the police would be forced to accept the theory of an invisible killer. It was my intention to rob a few banks — which I have done — and pad the money inside my suit, then make my getaway by plane to Europe. Before leaving, however, I should have killed Calthorp by poisoning him. I would have left a certain amount of the stolen money on him, enough to convince the police he was the invisible man. It would have looked like suicide to them, and the hunt would have been over, leaving an entirely unsuspecting world for me to prey upon. As for Sheila, she would have died too; but she is rather an attractive young lady for whom I have a great deal of admiration — physically. I would have spent rather a charming night with her prior to her, er, execution.'

Sheila shuddered, and Denby slipped an arm about her shoulders. Calthorp said, 'You won't get away with this, you know, Street. I'll find something to combat your devilishness . . . '

'I think not. You won't be alive to do anything, Doctor. Nor will your daughter or her friend here. I have it all planned. It will be a matter of the police finding all of you dead in your own home. It will be arranged to look as if you had gone insane and killed your daughter, and that you had been surprised by Mr. Collins and had killed him — but not before he had mortally wounded you!'

'You think for one minute they'd credit that?'

'Why not? They are already sure you are the invisible man. I don't enter into it at all. Oh, it will work, Doctor.'

His chuckle came eerily from empty air. He waved the gun negligently and said, 'I cannot be stopped now. Think what a priceless gift, Doctor, is the ability to see and remain unseen! I am unconquerable.'

'You are not *immortal*,' snapped Calthorp grimly. 'We must all die sooner or later — and I think your time will not be long.'

He stopped speaking, for Denby Collins had left the girl and was walking coolly towards the gun. Street rasped, 'Stay where you are!'

Denby halted a mere two feet in front of the red splotch which hovered in the air. His eyes were fixed slightly to the right of the visible wound, where the man's chin would have been had his face been visible. He said slowly, 'You're finished, Street. You're visible now — visible by the mark on your cheek! It's as good as seeing your entire face.'

'That can be remedied — after I have dealt with you three . . . '

Denby said, 'But you aren't in any position to deal with us three. That gun you hold *isn't loaded*. I fired every shot in it at you in madam's, and into the lock of this door!' He wasn't quite sure if he had; he couldn't recall whether he had fired three or four shots into the lock. If it had been three, *he* was the one who was finished. He gazed, fascinated, as the trigger on the gun started to move backwards; as the invisible finger tautened on it . . . Then his fist started to sweep forward, gauged to connect just right of that red splotch . . .

The trigger clicked uselessly one second before his blow drove home. Then he had the satisfying sensation of feeling bone crack beneath that terrible blow, and a solidness before him reeling backwards.

The red spot was now moving dazedly, a few inches above the floorboards. He threw himself recklessly onto it and started driving home hard, crushing blows. Unseen fingers hooked into his throat and caught his breath. A bony knee jabbed savagely into his stomach. He fought on in spite of the haze which was dancing about before his eyes.

Then suddenly there was nothing at all beneath him but the bare boards. He glanced up and saw the red splotch moving rapidly through the door. He struggled to his feet and gave chase . . .

The invisible man was almost as beaten as Denby; but the two kept going, down the path, into the road, and along it.

The red patch was a clearly visible stain of blood, fresh and glistening in the moonlight which shone down. Denby followed it doggedly, trying to put on more speed, trying to catch up before it

212

eluded him. They were approaching the crossroads when he did come to grips; he felt cloth beneath his hands, and braced himself to throw the other to the ground . . . The hard, battering force of a foot lashed his legs from under him, and he fell to his knees.

The invisible man laughed crazily and snarled: 'You can't stop me — no one can stop me! I'm invincible! I've got *brains*! I'll fool the entire country!' His foot crashed home on Denby's face again, driving the writer flat. The red splotch suddenly leaped from the pavement and started to speed across the road.

There was a squeal of raucous brakes, a horrified shout — and a thin, high scream!

Denby picked himself up and walked towards the centre of the road. He touched something with his foot. The driver of the heavy railway wagon alighted from his seat and came towards Denby. He said, 'Lumme, guv'nor, wot the 'ell did I 'it? I didn't see nuffin'! I didn't see nuffin' at all — just felt the jolt, like.'

'You hit that,' said Denby, pointing, and the driver's eyes widened in horror as they fell upon a man's head — just the top portion of it.

The driver gulped: 'Wh — where the 'ell's the rest of his body? 'ell, I 'aven't knocked his ruddy 'ead clean off, 'ave I?'

'You haven't. The rest of his body's invisible. Look.' He fumbled about for the tear in the headpiece of the dead man's garment. He found it and slowly tore it down. Gradually the weedy frame of Jack Street came to view.

'Lumme,' said the driver, 'I don't believe it. You reckon I'll get me licence suspended for this, guv? I couldn't see 'im at all.'

'You'll more likely get a reward,' Denby told him. He turned to Sheila and Calthorp, who had arrived and were staring down at the dead Street. Sheila shuddered, and Denby put an arm about her slim waist. He said, 'All's well . . . You know the rest. We'd better put through a call to Sharkey.'

★   ★   ★

Chief Inspector Sharkey removed the piece of matchstick from his teeth and seized the bride firmly in his plump arms. He then exercised his privilege of kissing her.

The affair of the Invisible Killer was at an end, had been almost forgotten by those concerned. A marriage had taken place between Denby Collins, writer, and Miss Sheila Calthorp, only daughter of Dr. Calthorp. Sharkey had been best man. The reception was almost over; the guests were streaming away. The happy couple were about to be left alone. Sharkey said, 'By the way, Doctor — about the invisible suit of yours. There should be some kind of law to prevent it falling into the wrong hands, you know.'

Calthorp smiled and said, 'Don't worry, Mr. Sharkey. The suit is destroyed — and so is the formula! I've had enough of the thing. No one will ever get their hands on it.'

Sharkey nodded, said his good-nights, and left. Doctor Calthorp went with him.

Denby kissed Sheila and said, 'To coin a phrase, alone at last!'

'Hadn't we better search the room before we come to that conclusion? How

215

do I know you haven't any invisible *women* tucked away here?'

Denby laughed. 'What on earth would I want with invisible women, dear? I'd much rather have them where I can see them.' She smiled and kissed him. He said, 'Sorry we can't have our honeymoon for a few weeks, but I must have this new book in the publisher's hands by the end of the month. You don't mind, do you, darling?'

'Of course not, Denby,' she told him. 'We can be happy here by ourselves, can't we, dear?'

'Hmm! Well, we won't quite be by ourselves. I do have a secretary.'

'Oh, I don't mind a young man about the place. Really.'

'It isn't exactly a young man, dear. You see — well, it's a woman. A — a girl, so to speak.'

'A *girl*?'

'Yes. An awfully good secretary. I told her some time ago I was marrying you if you'd have me. She said you'd get me to fire her; you'd be jealous. Silly, wasn't she?'

'Er — yes,' agreed Sheila rather thoughtfully. 'Hum, er, what's she like, Denby?'

'Eh? Oh, I don't know. Like a secretary, I suppose. I'll ring for her and introduce you if you like.'

He thumbed the bell, and Miss Volt entered bearing a copious selection of notes. She said, 'You rang, Mr. Collins?'

'Yes. I'd like you to meet Miss Volt, dear. This is my wife, Sheila.'

'How do you do,' said Sheila distantly.

'Not too badly, thanks,' responded Miss Volt, equally distant.

'That's all, Miss Volt,' said Denby faintly. Miss Volt left with a sniff. Sheila looked engrossed.

'That was Miss Volt, dear,' he told her.

'I noticed that, Denby. She — she isn't a bit like a secretary, is she? I mean she doesn't wear horn-rimmed glasses, nor black woollen stockings — and she isn't bad-looking, in a way.'

'I suppose not. Secretaries are like that these days.'

'Denby, couldn't you — for my sake — hire a *male* secretary?'

'But dear, Miss Volt knows me from top to bottom.'

'That,' said Sheila stiffly, 'is just what I'm afraid of! Oh, Denby, please . . . '

'Oh, hell,' said Denby, 'all right. You win, dear. Miss Volt will have no trouble getting another job.'

'Darling!' said Sheila.

THE END